A Dopeboy's Dream 2

Romell Tukes

Lock Down Publications and
Ca$h
Presents
A Dopeboy's Dream 2
A Novel by *Romell Tukes*

Lock Down Publications
P.O. Box 944
Stockbridge, Ga 30281
www.lockdownpublications.com

Copyright 2021 Romell Tukes
A Dopeboy's Dream 2

Lock Down Publications
Like our page on Facebook: Lock Down Publications @
www.facebook.com/lockdownpublications.ldp

Book interior design by: **Shawn Walker**
Edited by: **Jill Alicea**

Stay Connected with Us!

Text **LOCKDOWN** to 22828 to stay up-to-date with new releases, sneak peaks, contests and more…

Thank you!

Submission Guideline.

Submit the first three chapters of your completed manuscript to ldpsubmissions@gmail.com, subject line: Your book's title. The manuscript must be in a .doc file and sent as an attachment. Document should be in Times New Roman, double spaced and in size 12 font. Also, provide your synopsis and full contact information. If sending multiple submissions, they must each be in a separate email.

Have a story but no way to send it electronically? You can still submit to LDP/Ca$h Presents. Send in the first three chapters, written or typed, of your completed manuscript to:

LDP: Submissions Dept
P.O. Box 944
Stockbridge, Ga 30281

DO NOT send original manuscript. Must be a duplicate.

Provide your synopsis and a cover letter containing your full contact information.

Thanks for considering LDP and Ca$h Presents.

Acknowledgments

First and foremost, I want to give all praises to Allah the Most High. Thank you to all the readers in the streets, in prisons, or at work. Shout out to my family, my pops, love you, Smoke a.k.a. Moreno, love you, bro. Shout out to NY, Yonkers, we here YB, Lingo, CB, Kazzy, Smurf, Frasier, Banger, Baby James. Shout out OG Chuck from BK, shout out Marcus Clark, my VA fam, my DC brothers. Shout out to all the good brothers locked up behind these walls never coming home. Hold your head up, never give up, put your trust in Allah. To all the parents, let's raise our children correctly so they can be better. Big shout out to Cash. You're a mastermind, and I respect your thought process. Shout out Lockdown Publications, we in the building.

Romell Tukes

Prologue

Last Year

Don and Kay had the mean streets of Bad News, VA in a chokehold with their crew, Montay, Capo, Tech, and Lil' PJ.

Don and Kay had different fathers, but they were both raised in the slums. The brothers started off selling a little weed here and there, until they robbed and killed Gangsta, their aunt's boyfriend and a local kingpin. Gangsta was also the brother of Homo and Razor, whose names were heavy and VA. When they were killed, Gangsta sparked a new war in the city, leaving a lot of dead bodies. During the war, Don's mother introduced him to his pops, Rich, who he'd never met.

Rich was an ex-kingpin who was from New York but was getting money in VA. He ended up catching a life sentence in the commonwealth state for murder and drugs. His girl at the time, Bree, set him up. Bree and his brother, Big Bio, robbed him blind of all his bricks and money.

After a couple of visits, Don and Rich got closer and Rich offered his son a position within his ranks. Rich knew his son was out there getting a little money, but he had a plan to help him get rich.

Rich told Don he needed him and Kay, his brother, to link up with Big Bio and Bree, looking for a plug, and rock them to sleep, waiting on the perfect time to enforce their plan of revenge.

Don got together with Big Boi, and K got with Bree for a plug. Both brothers were getting money and locking down VA, although they were still warring with Homo and Razor.

When Montay got killed and then Razor, the city's murder rate rose. Capo and Lil' PJ were robbing and killing people from Big Boi and Bree's crew, but nobody knew where all the hits were coming from.

Bree got a lead on Tech, who was a friend of K's, and had her girl, Ivy, set him up to give him AIDS. Bree tried to get Tech to give up some information on who was aiming for her head. Tech stood his ground, not saying the word, losing his life that night for the sake of his guys.

As time passed, Big Boi's right hand, Melly, was watching him closely. He had a funny feeling Big Boi was playing both sides.

Captain Cole was a dirty cop who was extorting drug dealers and anybody with money. He was a snake willing to bite anybody for a dollar and found himself in the mix, exposing Don's crew.

Rick found out he was fucking Bree somehow, and told him to kill K, or his family's lives would be at risk, even after Don killed his own uncle, Big Boi, for Rich.

Leaving Don with no choice, he met up with his brother, K, and shot him, leaving him to die.

On K's way to the hospital, Bree killed all the EMT workers and told him she knew who he was and his objectives. She finished the job Don couldn't do.

The same night, Capo shot Melly in his face twice. When K's little brother, 50, made it to the hospital to see what was going on with K, he wished it was him in the hospital instead of his favorite brother.

When the doctor came out and told 50 his brother didn't make it, he cried. When Shay, his sister, came, she cried, going crazy.

Don went to go see Rich, who was now proud of him and told him it was time for him to meet Bree and finish a job.

50 ended up with Bri's best friend, Ivy, at her crib where he pistol-whipped her, and she told him everything about how

Don killed K and now Don was working for her. 50 wanted blood, and he was back to get it.

Romell Tukes

Chapter 1

Hampton, VA
Present

Don sat on the side of his pool watching two beautiful white women swim laps back and forth. One of them just got done sucking his dick in the water and didn't come up for air until he came.

Looking at his mansion, he couldn't help but think back to last year when he was living in the projects.

His 18,619-square-foot mansion was a beauty with six bedrooms, four-and-a-half bathrooms, a four-car garage, and balconies in each room. Brazil oak hardwood floors, an outdoor pool, private lounge, and four acres.

Don had a new red Audi R8 Spyder, a white Range Rover, and two motorcycles. Life was good and money was flowing better than ever in the past year since Bree had been supplying him.

The relationship he had with Bree was strictly business. There were a few times where he would go to her house in Dumfries and she would have on a two-piece bikini to seduce him.

Don stood his ground, focusing on business, and after a while, she gave up and had so much more respect for him. Bree looked down on a man who couldn't control his lust or desire, like Rich and K, which cost them their lives in some way.

Since he killed Big Boi, Don took over his spot in Fredericksburg and Alexandria.

His crew still had Bad News on lock, even though they had some new competition in the state. Don still had some ops in the streets who wanted his head, but he was always ready and so was his crew.

There wasn't a day that went by where he didn't miss his brother, K, but he knew there were rules to this game that had to be followed.

When he found out from Bree's own mouth that she was the one who killed K, he didn't know what to say.

Knowing he had to focus on money and the plan, he looked past it because most likely, K was going to die from his gun or Bree's gun.

He was happy K died at the hands of Bree instead of his. That took some weight off his shoulders. He remembered carrying K's casket with real tears from the guilt and seeing the pain in his mom, brother, and sister's faces.

He bought his mom a house to make up for the loss, and he paid his sister's college tuition. For some reason, 50, his little brother, was distant and doing his own thing, so Don let him be.

Don had a sit-down with Bree tonight to prepare for his next shipment in a couple of days. Don was only selling heroin a.k.a. dog food, which was major all over VA. He made over a million dollars in two months off dog food.

Checking his big-face Rolex, he climbed out the water, showing off his muscular upper body as his long dreads swung back and forth.

***

Fairfax, VA

Melly's mother, Sharee, was leaving her mini mansion, in a nice, quiet, upscale neighborhood, on her way to church. Six months ago, her son gave her a nice home and a nice car, but she already knew it was drug money.

Sharee was an upstanding church woman who devoted her life to God. Two months ago, her apartment burned down because her neighbor left gas on all night, causing a fire.

With no choice but to move in the mansion, Sharee moved in and was now loving every inch of the crib that used to belong to Melly until he recently moved to Norfolk, Virginia.

She was driving her Lexus truck listening to gospel music, getting in her morning church mood. A van with tint making a right onto the exit was coming at her full speed.

The van slammed into the driver's door, making Sharee's head bang onto her steering wheel, almost knocking her out. Two men snatched the beat-up door open and took her out, tossing her into the van, pulling off on a nice Sunday morning.

***

Bad News, VA

An hour later, Sharee was hog tied with thick rope and duct tape around her mouth, eyes, and head, leaving her nose open to breathe.

"Take that shit off her, dog," a male said, standing in front of Sharee, who was laying on the cold cement floor.

When the tape came off from across her face, Sharee saw three men with guns staring at her.

"Please, Jesus, my Lord and Savior, protect me from these evil, dangerous men," Sharee cried out before one of Lil' PJ's goons kicked her in her stomach with a pair of Timbs.

"Ahhhhhhhh…" she cried in pain, feeling her ribs crack.

"Last chance, bitch, where is he?" Lil' PJ asked in a serious tone.

Lil' PJ had been trying to catch Melly for months, but it was like he disappeared. When Lil' PJ got some info on a mini mansion in Fairfax, they only saw Sharee coming and going.

Once he saw Sharee, he knew she was Melly's mom. They looked just alike. This was his only way to Melly until he showed his face again.

"I will never give my son up to you devils. He is protected by Jesus," she screamed so loud, like a mad woman, her voice echoed.

"He may be, but you're not..."

Boc, Boc, Boc...

Lil' PJ killed her and walked out the old shed behind a middle school in the Ville projects.

Lil' PJ was running the streets getting a big bag, but it'd been quiet for a year-and-a-half, besides a little beef his crew had with Ja and Racks, the new crew in town from Richmond, Virginia.

Melly and Homo's names were popping up lately, and Lil' PJ was hunting them down. He refused to let them get away this time.

His crew was ready for another war, especially Capo and Pookie. But nobody knew what they were in for this go around.

Chapter 2

Bad News, VA

50 and his best friend, Tank Brim, posted up in the trap where they sold weed and molly.

In the last year, 50 and Tank Brim had been staying out of the way, focused on getting money. This guy definitely was plotting a plan to get at Don and his crew for the death of his brother.

"When are we going to bust that move, bro? I'm sick of selling this weak ass mid-green. This shit ain't even no loud," 50 told Tank Brim, who was in the room bagging up ounces of weed.

"I'ma see what's up, dawg, just give me some time. Are you sure you want to rob our plug, homie?" Tank Brim asked.

"Fuck yeah, nigga, I'm sick of selling nickel-and-dime. We can lock down this side of town and run it up, bro," 50 stated, getting up from cleaning his AK-47.

"Yeah, what about Ja and Racks? You know Ja going to be in his feelings if we kill his brother and lock down this whole west side. You already know they're going to be gunning for our heads," Tank Brim stated, while 50 opened a closet full of handguns, assault rifles, and submachine guns that were fully loaded.

"This is why we are war ready. What do you want a vest for a dog?" 50 stated, being funny.

"I ain't scared of nothing. I'm Fruit Town Brim, we don't fear nothing," Tank Brim stated, throwing up his set, making 50 laugh so hard he fell on the air mattress.

"Nah, bro, for real, we got to plan this shit out from A to Z," 50 stated.

"When you want to handle that Don situation?" Tank Brim asked, knowing this was a touchy topic.

"When the time is right, because he don't have a clue we know what's up, so let's focus on this move then focus on them niggas," 50 replied, seeing a text from his wife, Jazzy.

"Aight." Tank Brim went back to bagging up the weed he plan to give to his little cousin to sell for him.

Tank Brim was in his early twenties, tall, and dark skin, with dreads, tattoos on his face, and a nice muscular build from years of football in high school. He was like 65% of young African Americans raised in the hood. His mom was a fiend, his father was a deadbeat, and he was trying to keep his head above water.

50 was his best friend since they were kids, they even called each other brothers. The friends were ready to up their game and cross over to the dog food where the real money was at.

***

SUX 2 Prison, VA

Rich was inside the prison gym working out, doing his regular 20 sets of pull-ups, dips, and push-ups, twenty reps each.

The workout had Rich sweating with his shirt off, showing his well-defined back, arms, and chest. Rich was flexing on niggas because he was in his early forties looking better than most niggas in their twenties who exercised all day.

Two of his personal bodyguards posted up on the wall, protecting Rich.

The prison was a maximum-security jail, and prisoners were getting stabbed, jumped by other prisoners, raped, robbed, extorted, and used as drug mules.

Rich had the jail on lock, getting all the drugs, phones, and contraband. Most loved Rich and some hated him, but they were too scared to approach him because they knew how he was coming.

There were over 60 niggas from New York in the jail because they got caught up in VA for trying to sell drugs or scam.

This past weekend, Don came up to see him to inform him how things were going. Rich was starting to build a father-son relationship with Don, and it felt good.

Growing up, Rich never really had his father around, so he figured he could be a good father figure to Don by showing him the game.

Rich knew if he would have known everything then that he knew now, he wouldn't be in prison listening to niggas' war stories all day.

Finishing up his last set, he saw a fist fight pop off on the other side of the gym. A big stocky dude from Yonkers, New York knocked out a skinny, tall nigga with gold teeth from Richmond.

The Richmond dude gathered up around the New York dude who pulled out a knife, ready to work.

"Ayo..." one of Rich's goons shouted as everybody looked toward Rich and his goons, who niggas feared, as they approached them.

"Yo, we got a problem, son?" Rich said, looking at the head nigga from Richmond who was getting money in the jail.

"Nah, bruh, we good. Your boy robbed my little man of two hundred worth of commissary. You know it's about respect," Big Grumpy stated.

"He took this shit in his face or behind his back?" Rich said, looking at the skinny dude finally wake up, unaware of what just happened.

"He took it in front of his face in his cell," Big Grumpy stated, knowing if a nigga got robbed and ain't do shit, then it was fair game.

"Well, if that's what type of nigga you dealing with, then maybe you should change your company. Yo, Eagle, come on," Rich said, calling the nigga from New York as the VA got his way, hoping he didn't cut one of them in the face.

Rich walked off talking to Eagle, letting him know if he was fucked up or needed something, he could have holla'd at him. Because New York moved as one whenever they were out of state.

Rich gave Eagle 8 oz of dog food and $500 worth of food. Rich had so much food, he had to use nine niggas' cells to store it.

***

Manassas, VA

Homo was in a hole-in-the-wall strip club alone, drinking liquor bottle after bottle, getting fucked up.

The past year, Homo had been getting money in PG County, Maryland with his cousin who lived out there in the hood, getting a little crack money. Homo went out there with some keys and found a connect, but he was now back in VA for one reason and one reason only.

Don was on his hit list when he got away from the city because it was too hot. The only names he was hearing all over VA were Bree, CL, and Don.

Homo was on a serious mission, and he wasn't going to let Don slip this time. He put his life on it.

Chapter 3

Bad News, VA

Melly's mom's funeral was packed today with family and friends. The death of his mom sparked a new savage inside of Melly.

He sat in the front row with a pair of dark Cartier shades on, looking at his mother's casket. His grandma was sitting next to him, in tears. He'd been trying his best to console her, but he was going through his own emotional roller coaster.

After the funeral, Melly watched the crowd clear out and sent his grandma home in a limousine with his aunts and uncles.

"Yo, Melly," a voice said, walking up to him.

"CL, what's good?"

"Ain't shit, bruh, just came from visiting my grandma's grave down the hill." CL looked at Melly's attire and liked his style.

CL always had his eyes on Melly because he was a hustler. He knew Big Bio was killed in DC, so he knew Melly needed a plug. CL heard about Melly's mom being killed, so he knew Melly would be back in town.

CL's grandma was still alive, he just lied to make it not look strange for him to come talk about business.

"How's everything?"

"Shit, good, I'm just out here grindin', always looking for the next best takeover." CL looked in the sky, trying his best not to be so obvious he was talking about Melly.

"Is that right? I've been outta town getting money, but I'll be out here for a while, and I still got some men out here getting money," Melly stated, catching on to CL's statement.

"Maybe I can help with that. I'm still in business. Sometime next week, stop by my furniture store so we can talk about it on Main Street." CL would talk and put it in his plan A.

Melly walked to his car thinking about his talk with CL. He always used to see him around, and he used to see him when Big Boi would meet with him to re-up.

This was big, but Melly couldn't lose his focus on Don and his crew. He heard they were doing big things in the city, but Melly's plan was to put a stop to all of that. He left the graveyard with Don and money on his mind.

***

West Bad News, VA

Frenchy was one of the head dope boys on the west side of the city. He was Ja's younger brother. Frenchy had pounds of weed, molly, bricks of coke, and lean for sale. He was flooding the west area of the town.

"You got that money from last night you owe, right?" Frenchy asked Grain, who just walked out of one of the apartment complexes he was selling drugs out of.

"Huh..." Grain wished he would have gone out the back exit and through the backdoor basketball court. He owed Frenchy three thousand dollars he didn't have.

"Nigga, you ain't deaf." Frenchy pulled out his pistol. *Whack!!*

Frenchy slapped Grain so hard with his Glock he almost did a double backflip. There were five niggas posted up outside watching Grain get pistol-whipped, and one of them was his cousin.

"You remember now, fuck nigga?" Frenchy shouted, standing over Grain, sending vicious blows to his head until he wasn't moving.

"Yeah, fuck boy," Frenchy yelled, spitting on him. "Clean this sorry ass nigga up. Get him off the block before them boys roll through here." Frenchy walked off to his car.

Frenchy lived across the bridge next to the city hall and library. He had a nice apartment with his baby mother and four-year-old son.

He tried to provide a good lifestyle for his baby mother and child, and selling drugs was only for the time being.

Once at his building, he parked in the front, looking over his shoulder as he did every night before walking in his crib. The streets were dangerous in VA. It was normally the ones closest to you who would kill you for power and position.

Walking through the lobby, he saw his mailbox left wide open with the mail still inside it, like someone was in a rush and forgot to close it.

Frenchy couldn't wait to curse Gabrielle out for leaving the mailbox open when he got upstairs.

He called out for Gabriella as he entered the apartment, closing the door behind him. An instant later, he felt the cold barrel of a gun pressed to the side of his head. His mind went straight to the stash of money that he kept behind his bathroom mirror. *Damn*, he thought, *I'ma have to come off my dough or I'ma die.*

"Take it easy, bro. I got whatever you want, just don't harm me or my family most of all," Frenchy stated, scared.

"Nigga, walk," Tank Brim said with a red flag wrapped around his face, forcing Frenchy into the living room area.

Stepping foot into the living room, 50 was standing over his baby mother and son tied up on the floor.

Frenchy's heart went out to his family, but he knew if worse came to worse, then he would have to put his life first.

"Where's the money and drugs at, Frenchy? And let's not play reindeer games, dog," Tank Brim said.

"Tank Brim." Frenchy recognized the voice. 50 slapped Frenchy with the butt of the TEC-9 submachine gun.

"Ahhhhhhh...."

"It's nothing here. Tank/ I can't believe you crossing me, cuz, after all the love I showed you, bro." Frenchy rubbed the side of his head.

"Who do you love the most?" Tank Brim looked at his family then back to Frenchy.

"My son, why?"

Boc, Boc...

50 shot his son in the head, leaving two small holes with blood pouring out. Frenchy and his baby mother started crying.

"Everything is in the bathroom behind the large mirror. I swear on everything, bro."

50 took him to the bathroom where he saw a large mirror in the shower. Frenchy opened the mirror by pushing it in. As the mirror popped out, a safe was behind it. He punched in the code for 50, and stacks of bricks and money were inside.

"I don't care about her, bro, just let me go..." Frenchy begged.

50 believed he never saw such a fuck nigga. 50 shot Frenchy eight times, watching his body fall into the large tub. 50 grabbed everything in his arms, then he heard two shots and ran outside to see Frenchy's baby mother shot in the head. "She was moving too much," Tank Brim said, helping 50 load everything into backpacks.

Chapter 4

Bad News, VA

"You thought we wouldn't catch you, dawg?" Pookie said, standing in Weezy's crib, looking at him tied up on the floor.

"Don't do me like this, bro. Please, it's only a half a key. I swear on everything my dog ate it, cuz, I swear on my momma's grave," Weezy screamed.

"Nigga, who the fuck I look like?" Pookie said, putting his gun down and pulling out a blade.

"Call Don, cuz, he knows I'm good for it, bro," Weezy stated, seeing the blade, knowing how crazy Pookie was.

He'd heard vicious stories about Pookie a while back, so when he saw him standing in his building, he tried to run.

Pookie chased him down and pistol-whipped him, then dragged him into his apartment.

"Don sent me here, fuck boy, so your wild cards ran out." Pookie rammed the knife into Weezy's eye.

"Ahhhhhhh….." he screamed.

Pookie sliced his neck wide open and started ramming the sharp blade in and out his heart, kidneys, and liver.

This wasn't Pookie's first time stabbing a man to death. He knew when the body went limp the victim was dead, and Pookie made the crime scene hard for the pathologist to establish how his victims died.

Pookie sat on Weezy's couch next to the dead body to take a smoke break. Pookie was Don's friend and hitman.

A couple of months ago, Pookie just got out of a mental hospital in Richmond where he spent two years after biting a judge's ear in court.

Pookie acted crazy, but he was very smart and well educated. His mother was a college professor, and his father was a pastor for a big church.

If someone would have a regular conversation with him, they would never know he was off. At 20 years old, he was one of the craziest killers a city had ever seen.

Pookie was dark, tall, ugly, and had a mouth full of gold, but some women found his strange style attractive.

It was time to leave, and his father wanted him to come to pray at night at the church. Pookie didn't believe in a higher power, but he was only going so his dad could stop asking him.

***

Norfolk, VA

Roc and Twin were driving around the city of Norfolk on their way to meet two bad bitches they flew out from LA. They met a couple of weeks ago when Roc and Twin went to Cali.

The two brothers had been back and forth from Norfolk to Bad News getting big money with the new connect they met in LA six months ago. They stopped fucking with Bree when they found out she was supplying Don. Both of the brothers warned Bree about dealing with Don, but she was not hearing it.

Don was bringing her so much money she refused to cut him off because Roc and Twin disliked him. Now Rock and Twin were both moving big weight thanks to their crip plug from Grape Street in the Watts.

There wasn't a day that went by where they weren't thinking about killing Don and his crew. Don and his boys were the talk of Bad News, and Roc and Twin were sick of it. They had a plan to take over what should have been theirs.

***

North Bad News, VA

Ja was mourning the loss of his little brother, Frenchy. He was appalled to hear about his death, because his brother was a good kid just trying too hard to be something he wasn't.

Ja was a big-time dope boy, and his connect was his cousin, CL. Ja was 27 years old and he'd been in the game since he was 13.

Ja was a businessman. He owned a trucking company with his cousin, Racks, who just came home from prison. While Ja was using his trucking company to move drugs around, Racks was in the streets in the middle of everything.

Ja hadn't found out who killed his brother yet, but Frenchy's neighbor told Racks she saw two men leaving his apartment. For anyone to kill a kid and an innocent woman, Ja knew he was about to go up on some animals, and he hoped Racks was ready.

Ja answered the company phone in his office, writing down the certain 18 wheeler his customer was on the phone requesting.

***

Dale City, VA

Jazzy turned over on her California king-size bed so her boyfriend, 50, could hit it from the back. She obediently got on her knees at his request.

50 started stroking in and out of her tightness. He snatched her hair, compelling her to arch her back and bring her pelvis further back unto his manhood.

"Uggghhh, yesss..." Jazzy moaned, feeling his balls slap against her thighs.

The couple had been fucking for so long tonight the Ne-yo CD played over twice in the surround sound system.

"I'm cumming...." 50 couldn't hold himself any longer as she made her coochie walls grip and massage his shaft.

Jazzy already reached her orgasm, so she was tapped out, but she was trying to be a team player.

"Fuck, babe." 50 lay down, looking at her perfect teeth, watching her blush.

"What?" she asked him as he stared into her deep eyes, pushing her goldish hair back behind her big ears that he loved.

Jazzy was sexy as hell to him, and being the same age, they connected mentally. They'd been together for three years almost, on and off, but the love was real.

Jazzy's real name was Jessica, and she went to Norfolk State University studying to become a forensic biologist. She had her own crib and car, so she needed nothing from no nigga.

"I'ma be back in two days. Keep that back here and don't touch it," he stated seriously.

"Babe, I will never go against what you say," she said, kissing his lips, leaning to him because she looked in the back twice to see a lot of money.

She wasn't a dumb girl. She grew up in the hood, so there was nothing 50 could do to trick her into believing he was a good, tax-paying citizen.

Chapter 5

Sux 2 Prison, VA

Rich was in his cell taking his 11 a.m. nap while two of his men stood guard outside his cell with big blades, just in case anybody had an idea.

Earlier, he fucked a CO bitch in his cell while most of the unit was outside on the yard or at work. The woman sucked his dick so good he wanted to marry her.

Being in prison wasn't so bad for Rich, only because he had a bag. He was making at least $25,000 a week with all the shorts from the jailhouse drug dealers.

Rich even had the warden eating out of his hand. He was the reason why she just bought a new house and put her son through college.

Eagle knocked on Rich's door, waking him up.

"Yo, boss, you got a visit." Eagle closed the door and continued to post up like he was a National Guard.

Rick knew Don was supposed to come up this week, but he didn't know it would be today.

Getting out of bed, he wished he could go back to sleep. Shawty put it on him so good earlier he couldn't even walk.

After brushing his teeth and washing his face, he was about ready.

Rich walked to the unit, seeing a couple of inmates watching his every move, ready to drop a slip to the captain and snitch, letting the people know who was selling drugs and fucking corrections officers.

Prisoners dropped slips on Rich every day, but nobody knew he had everybody in the higher ranks on a monthly payroll.

"Have a good visit, Rich. I hope you ain't got no bitch coming to see you," a female CO said, serious, because she was the one sucking his pole earlier.

"Nah, but if I did, you would be the first to hear about it, Superhead," he stated, making her blush with embarrassment.

Don was sitting in the back at his regular table. His dad had so much power in the jail, he had his own table.

"Don, what's up, my boy?" Rich greeted his son, who had a worried look on his face.

"How are you holding up?"

"The best I can, champ. I'm sick of these country bamas," Rich stated, forgetting his son was a VA baby.

"Damn, I'm country too," Don said.

"No the hell you're not, kid. You got my blood in you and that's pure New York shit." Rich was serious about this.

"What happened with the appeal lawyer?" Don asked about the appeal lawyer he hired to file a motion of appeal for his father to get his time back.

"The courts denied me, Don. You keep forgetting I'm a New Yorker in a commonwealth state who took over the drug trade and killed some people in the mix. I may not see daylight again, but I can live with it now. Enough about me, why the long face?"

"We got a problem. Bree ain't answering her phone," Don stated.

"She may be on vacation, got a new number, sucking dick, or out of town somewhere, don't worry," Rich replied.

"Nah, something ain't right. I went by her spot and she was long gone. You think she's on to us?" Don asked.

"Hell no, nigga, Bree may look smart and act smart, but the bitch is slow. You did everything right. She will never assume nothing, you cover your tracks too well." Rich knew

Bree must have moved or just didn't feel like being bothered at the moment for whatever reason.

"I am looking more into it, bro. I got a feeling something ain't right. I need to re-up. I'm down to my last 20," Don stated, seeing Rich was in deep thought.

"This is why I always tell you to be up when you hit your last 50 birds that sit low," Rich added to school him.

"I know, but she wasn't picking up, and I don't really know what to do now, dog."

"Just chill, if she don't pick up or reach out to you in two weeks, I got something for you. The cut is 50/50 until I can find you a new connect," Rich said.

"I bet that, Pops, thanks." Don was happy now his pops had a plan B and C.

$$***$$

Bad News, VA

"Can you please hurry the fuck up, dog? I got six beans blowing my phone up, cuz," Meek shouted into the back so his friend Self God could hurry up.

The village projects were seeing major paper since Lil' PJ flooded the hood with the best heroin the city had ever seen in years.

"My bad, let's go," Self God stated as he placed a quarter key of dog food in his book bag.

The doorbell rang, taking both men out of the zone.

Meek looked into the peep hole to see a black cop with his work standing outside with a piece of paper.

"Yo, it's the police, bro," Meek said

"Fuck." Self God took off his book bag and placed it under the couch.

Neither of the men had warrants, but Meek did have some backup child support.

"How are you doing, Officer?" Meek asked before the cop blew his head off his frail shoulders.

Self God grabbed his gun off the living room table and fired two rounds toward the door. The cop dropped and rolled into the house, jumping up, firing four shots into Self God's chest, killing him.

The cop walked out the crib the same way he came in. The cop uniform and hat was something Homo came up with days ago. He knew how niggas got when the police came around.

Homo knew this was one of Lil' PJ's spots, so he just wanted to send a message.

Chapter 6

Bad News, VA

Lil' PJ and Pookie were chilling in the parking lot smoking and drinking with some bitches from the hood.

"You holler at Capo?" Pookie asked Lil' PJ, who was talking to a dark-skin chick from Atlanta who recently moved to Bad News.

"Hell na, bruh, that nigga called me trying to make me kill some bitch he fucking because she cheating. He's gonna tell me he don't wanna do it himself because he's gonna look sus," Lil' PJ stated, picking up a bottle of Grey Goose.

"Man, you know bruh be bugging out sometimes," Pookie stated as they walked to his car, leaving the women and their homies.

"You heard about Homo killing some of Capo's people?" Lil' PJ took a sip out the bottle.

"Nah... That's why he bugging out, dawg," Pookie stated.

"You know it's about to be a war zone as soon as Don finds out what happened." PJ knew Don had been waiting for Homo and Melly to surface again, but he was so focused on getting to a bag he was somewhat side tracked.

"Knowing him, he already did, bruh, but I gotta go holler at my pops. You know how he is." Pookie shook his head.

"You spend twenty-plus years in the army special ops or whatever he did, you'd be burned out too," Lil' P. stated, laughing but serious, because his little cousin's father spent ten years overseas and came back bugged out.

"I spent enough time in nut houses. Nigga on crazy meds, so I guess I'm burned out too," Pookie said, getting inside his car.

"You don't know the half, but tomorrow Don wants to meet with us, so be there, bruh. I love you," Lil' PJ said before walking off.

Pookie pulled off listening to soft jazz. It was something he always did to get him in a mellow mood.

When Pookie was away, Lil' PJ used to visit him daily and bring him things to free his mind, while Don and Capo used to hold him down on the money tip.

The love he had for Lil' PJ was raw, and he would do anything for him. He considered Lil' PJ a real brother.

***

Across Town

Pastor Ryan waited in the front row of his empty church, saying a silent prayer for his family, church members, friends, and all the people he killed.

He was in his mid forties, dark, and tall, with a bald head, muscular build, and one gold tooth. Pastor Ryan spent most of his youth in boot camps and the army, where he became a gun specialist and a trained killer.

With six tours and twenty-one medals of honor, he served his country well and was proud of it.

He came back from the last war with a fake leg because of a bomber in Syria.

Pastor Ryan hated street punks, low lifes, drug dealers, pimps, and most of all, gang bangers. He was determined to bring Pookie into the house of the Lord to become a devoted Christian.

The streets played a big part in Pookie's life. He only wished his son would see the light before it was too late.

Pookie walked through the door of the church high as a kite with a pair of sunglasses on.

When his father saw him, he almost had a heart attack smelling the weed and liquor on his breath.

"You come into the house of the Lord smelling like the devil's work," Pastor Ryan stated.

"I'm here, ain't I?" Pookie wasn't trying to hear his father's mouth.

"Son, I want you to get your life together. There is nothing in these streets for you. I raised you better than this." His father had a Holy Bible in his hand while talking.

"Father, you know I'm living a life of sin, but when I'm ready to give my life to God, Allah, or Budda, I will. I just want you to understand my heart isn't there, Pops. I'm sorry." Pookie was serious. One thing he refused to do was play with God at any level.

"I respect and understand that, but know when he calls for you on Judgment Day, there will be no second chance," Pastor Ryan explained, hoping his son would see the real picture that this was only a test and Pookie was failing.

"I'm willing to accept my faith as a man," Pookie said, seeing his dad's face frown.

"A man, what is a man? You not no damn man. I'll tell you what a man is, boy. A man is God-fearing, a man submits his soul and life to God, a man takes care of his family, a man doesn't play in the streets, a man lives on morals and honor. You think because you know how to use a gun or sell dope you're a man? You got a lot to learn about being a man," Pastor Ryan stood to leave.

Pookie sat there for five minutes getting his thoughts together before leaving the church he was raised in.

***

Downtown, DC.

Bree was in an upscale, classy hotel in the jacuzzi, drinking wine out a glass, relaxing her nerves.

Three weeks ago, Bree got word from a cop on her payroll that the feds were in town. When she met with Cap Cole, he informed her the feds and marshals were in town for her but mainly her Virginia Beach crew she had selling dope and warring within the city.

Bree knew money and killing were going to bring the feds, but she was enjoying the show and the feeling of power.

The feds already picked up nineteen of her workers and half of them told on her.

Bree wasn't on the indictment, she was just the main topic for the feds' case. They had nothing on her, but she knew they weren't going to stop at anything to get her.

Tomorrow, she was driving outta town to start over fresh. She had lots of money and drugs, so starting over in a new city was nothing to her.

Leaving Don and her other clients back was easy. She knew they would find a new plug someway. She just knew it wasn't going to be her any more.

Chapter 7

Tyson Corner, VA

Twin and his new girlfriend, Rihanna, were out shopping in the local mall. Rihanna was a pretty woman with a nice body who caught everybody's eye.

Before she met Twin and he started tricking on her, she was a regular hood bitch, busted and ratchet.

Twin sent her to get her body done in Miami, and she came back looking like a dime piece.

"I'm glad we came out today, babe, because a bitch need some new shoes," she said, looking at all the high heels on the wall inside the Chanel store.

"A bitch needs to get a job," Twin shot back, joking with her. He had no problem spending 20,000 on her, but sometimes she would blow 20,000 in one day on clothes, shoes, and dumb shit.

"I can go back to twerking on the pole. I bet niggas would love to see this phat ass slide up and down that pole," she said, poking her ass out as a couple of niggas looked, getting turned on.

"Stop playing with me, shawdy." Twin got serious, making her laugh.

"That's what I thought. Now come pay for these shoes so we can leave. I can't wait for you to smut me out tonight. I'm so horny," she moaned, which was like music to his ears, because so was he.

After getting his nut off, Twin would meet up with Roc later in Bad News to re-up because they were getting low on work.

***

Bad News, VA

Racks just got back from a big Go-Go party in DC, the Georgetown area. He had a slim, dark-skin chick with dreads with him bagged.

Racks was Ja's cousin, and he was getting some real money all through VA.

He spent most of his life in prison, and at the age of twenty-nine, he had two bids under his belt.

His last bid he did was seven years, and he just came home months ago to a big bag.

The streets were in his heart, it was all he knew. He loved everything about it except prison and death.

Racks was a pretty boy, light-skin nigga with long braids and a clean face. The women worshipped him and the ground he walked on.

As he was walking to the elevator, it stopped and the door opened. Two men with guns jumped out and grabbed Racks and the girl he was with, tossing them into the elevator.

Racks saw the men had no masks on, and he'd seen one of their faces before.

"This is going to be nice and easy," said Capo, with his Glock 17 pressed Racks' head..

"I don't want no problems. I have drugs and money inside, dog, just don't hurt us." Racks' heart was racing as he stepped off the elevator.

Pookie had his gun to the woman's back, listening to her sob and cry nonstop.

Inside the apartment, it was big with high ceilings and nice carpet.

"Everything is in my office room behind the file cabinet. It's a hole-in-the-wall where all the money and drugs are in two separate bags," Racks told them, to get a good look at Pookie.

"What the fuck you looking at, my nigga?" Pookie asked him.

"Nothing…" Racks said, seeing Capo walk off, going to the back rooms.

Two minutes later, Capo came out from the back with two bags, just as Racks said.

"Thanks for being a good team player, but is she your wifey?" Capo asked, looking at the woman's fat camel toe print.

"Nah, just a friend, but y'all got what y'all came for, so just leave us be, dawg," Racks stated with his frail chest out.

Capo nodded his head at Pookie, and he shot the woman in the back of the head.

"Have fun cleaning this shit up," Pookie said, laughing, walking out the apartment.

***

Hampton, VA

Capo was doing his aunt a favor and picking up his little cousin from summer school in Hampton, the inner city.

He parked his Benz sitting on 22-inch rims. Capo jumped out to see a teacher waving him down from his left side as he was trying to walk into the school.

"Sir, I'm sorry, but you can't park there," the beautiful teacher, who was Spanish with flawless bronze skin and nice eyes, said.

Capo was dazed by her beauty. She was making hand gestures in his face, trying to get his attention.

"I'm sorry, I'll move right now…" Capo saw her smiling. His little cousin came running out of school, jumping into her favorite cousin's arms.

"Hey, Ms. Rivera," Capo's little cousin told her home-room teacher.

"Hey, Biancca, enjoy your weekend," Ms. Rivera told Capo, seeing Biancca get in his car.

"I can't help it, you're beautiful and I want to take you on a date if you let me."

"You're brave, I like that, but no," she replied, turning to leave.

"Ok, wait, can we go to lunch one day?" Capo made her laugh, because he wasn't taking no for an answer.

"Next Friday, be here at 1 p.m.," Ms. Rivera said, walking off. Capo took a look at her perfect round ass.

Chapter 8

Richmond, VA

Don was in the private area of the upscale strip club, watching two thick, brown-skin dancers twerk. Don was drinking Dom P out the bottle, enjoying his night.

This was meditation to him. He had a truck full of goons waiting outside.

Don liked this strip club because it had private show rooms for the guests to have sex if the strippers were down.

One of the dancers climbed on his lap and grinded on his hardened pole.

"I want to suck this," she said, grabbing a handful of his manhood.

"What's stopping you?" Don asked, looking at her full lips. He was still watching the other women dance in front of him.

The woman pulled his cock out and did her thing, using her long tongue to taste him before she gulped his whole shaft.

When Don saw her swallow his whole meat, he was in love. She bopped her head back and forth while massaging his balls with her long nails.

Unable to hold on any longer, he shot a load down her throat, and she drank it like a pro.

Don was still excited. That's when the woman pushed her thong to the side and sat on Don's pole in reverse cowgirl position.

"Ugh…" she moaned, grinding slow as he opened her pussy walls. The other woman sucked on her girl's clit and Don's balls.

Don gripped her hips and took control, fucking her hard and rough, making her scream all types of curse words.

When the sex session was over, Don tried to give both women $2,000, but they refused. Don gave them his number and told them to call whenever.

He left the club with many thoughts on his mind as he made his way to Bad News.

Don heard Bree skipped town because the feds were on her radar. He only hoped the feds weren't on his trail, but he'd only been dealing with Bree for some months.

Everything Don did, he did it smartly, so the feds would never have a reason to build a case on him. His number one rule was not talking on the phone, which he learned from many dope boyz' downfalls.

Tomorrow, he planned to have a sit-down with his dad so Rich could hit him with some keys of dope until he found a solid plug.

***

Arlington County Jail, VA

Ashley was at work doing her regular rounds, going from unit to unit. She was a captain at the jail and the baddest white bitch in the jail.

Ashley worked six days a week. All her kids were grown, so she lived her life and did what she pleased.

Don and 50 were both her heart, but she knew they were going down the wrong path in life. She would talk to them all the time, but she couldn't get through to them.

Every day, she prayed for them to not end up like the prisoners she saw every day coming back and forth to jail.

Introducing Don to his father was the worst mistake she knew she made, because Rich was a bad role model. Since Don met his dad, Ashley saw something different in her son. She only hoped he saw the light before it got too dark and he lost sight forever. She walked in the unit and all eyes were on her. Prisoners loved when she came around with her fat ass.

***

Dale City, VA

Twin and Rihanna were driving through a small path leading into some woods, where people went hiking, camping, and to get a fresh peace of mind.

"Baby, why do we have to go hiking? That's white people shit. Let's go to Miami or Atlanta and turn up," Rihanna said, putting bug spray on her arms.

She'd never been hiking or into the whole wildlife thing. She thought it was overrated and for white people.

"You got to learn to try new shit and get out the hood, shorty." Twin parked and hopped out the truck, ready for a day of hiking.

"I guess one day of this bullshit won't hurt." Rihanna got out of the truck and followed his lead up a trail, going deep into the woods. It was still daylight out, so they had enough time to get a couple of hours of hiking in.

After an hour of walking through the hills, woods, and lakes, Rihanna was tired and upset. "I want to go back, baby. It's no life out here, and I don't have any service out here, baby," she cried out.

Twin had a shotgun with him for wild animals and bears, of course, because it was mating season, and bears could get very aggressive while in heat.

"You don't have to worry about going back," Twin said, making her turn around because she was about to go off on him.

When she saw the shotgun pointed at her face, her heart raced, seeing death in front of her.

BOOM...

The shotgun blast put a large hole through her face as her body fell in a small ditch.

Twin left her there and took her phone and purse. Twin had been waiting for this day since he found out from Roc that she was Lil' PJ's sister. Roc used to fuck Rihanna back in the day also before they started selling drugs. Twin couldn't wait until Lil' PJ heard about this.

***

Bad News, VA

Cap and Cole were driving around looking for any dealers who were on Bree's payroll, to take what she owed.

When he heard Bree skipped town, he was on fire because she was his main source of income.

She'd been paying him good for years, and then with her going, a lot of drug dealers were going to be without a plug. So, that meant a lot of dope boys were going to be coming up short on their monthly payment.

Cap and Cole saw one of Bree's workers walking down the street. He pulled onto the curb, almost hitting him.

When the man saw Cap and Cole's faces, he took off running like a slave chasing freedom.

Cole didn't feel like running after no low-level drug dealer, and he knew where the man lived.

He had another deal on his radar, and he knew this was a replacement for Bree's absence.

Chapter 9

Virginia Beach, VA

CL had a nice beach house he came to just to get away. Today he was meeting with Melly to have a sit-down. CL always liked Melly's style. He was a loyal soldier and he knew how to get to a bag.

There was a soft knock at the front door.

CL had a glass door throughout the house. He saw Melly standing there in a pair of sunglasses.

"Come in, bro, good to see you. Make yourself at home," CL said, letting him inside, walking into the living room.

"Thanks for inviting me. This spot is crazy fly." Melly looked around before sitting down in the all black-and-white living room.

"You want something to drink?"

"Yeah, you got D'ussé?" Melly asked.

"Yolanda... Two bottles of D'ussé," CL shouted to his maid in the kitchen making the men lunch.

"How's business?" Melly asked.

"Great, trying to stay on my grind. You've been off the map for a while now. Sometimes that's the best thing to do, especially with all these new niggas out here toe stepping," CL stated while his maid came out in a bikini, showing her phat ass and big titties with no stomach.

Melly couldn't help but look at the sexy, thick, Korean woman. He wondered where CL found her.

"You like that, shoot your shot later. It's a free game," CL told him.

"Since Big Boi got killed, I have been getting money out of town, but now I'ma be out here for a while. I need a new connect because I'm coming for what's mine." Melly's tone was serious.

CL popped his bottle and took a sip of the dark liquor, and Melly did the same thing.

"Are you sure you're ready to jump back in the field out here?"

"Them niggas killed my mother. I have no choice," Melly repeated.

"Aight, I'm with you Melly, just because I like your style. Whatever you need, I'm here for you. I look forward to a bright future for us," CL stated.

"Cheers to that," Melly said, holding up his bottle to tap it with CL's bottle. They further talked about drug payments and transactions.

***

Bad News, VA
1 Week Later

Lil' PJ was in a crowded church with family members and friends, who all were there attending his sister's funeral.

The same day his sister was killed, Capo called him telling him he saw Rihanna in a truck with Twin.

When Lil' PJ tried to call her that night, her phone was going to voicemail. Two days later, he got the call saying Rihanna's body was found in the woods, being eaten apart by mountain lions.

Lil' PJ sat in the back as Pastor Ryan, who was Pookie's father, gave the amazing sermon.

He couldn't build up the guts to stand in front of his sister's closed-casket service. Rihanna's face had a big hole in it and her body parts were chewed up badly, where a person could see the flesh.

Lil' PJ held back his tears and thought of a revenge plan to get Twin and Roc back. He didn't plan on sleeping until he saw blood spill the right way for Rihanna's gruesome death.

***

Stafford, VA

Capo's grandma Shirley was out paying bills this morning since it was the first of the month.

She still lived in the projects because she was comfortable there and it was where she'd lived her whole life.

Shirley knew what her grandson did for a living and she warned him, he was playing on the devil's playground. She was a church-going woman and raised her kids and grandkids in the house of the Lord.

Her last stop was the antique store and bargain stores.

Parking in her normal spot in the old Cadillac she had for ten years now, she got out.

A blue BMW pulled up to the side of her blasting loud music early in the morning. She shook her head at the new reckless generation.

When she saw the man get out of his car with a gun, she got back inside her car, but not fast enough.

Boc...

Boc...

Boc...

The three gunshots to her back made her fall inside, crying in pain.

Homo stood behind her and shot her two more times in the back of her head before climbing back in the BMW, racing off.

***

Bad News, VA

Meanwhile, Roc was leaving the Clinic Medical Center because he recently fucked a bitch he met in Hampton, and he couldn't stop itching.

He went for a checkup to find out he had crabs for the second time. Roc was pissed. He knew better than to go in Anna raw, but her sex box was so good he had to test the waters.

Outside, he walked down the street, then out of the corner of his eye, he saw a man running across the street with a gun.

Bloc...

Bloc...

Bloc...

Bloc...

Bloc...

Bloc...

Bloc...

Car windows shattered as Lil' PJ tried to take Roc's head off.

Roc pulled out his gun while ducking bullets and fired a couple of shots back. Two people were laid out on the floor, dead.

Boc...

Boc...

Boc...

Lil' PJ ducked the bullets and tried to get closer to Roc, but he was backpedaling into a parking lot.

Cop sirens could be heard. Lil' PJ fired four more shots, hitting Roc in his forearms, before running off, not trying to go to jail.

Chapter 10

Bad News, VA

50 recently bought a nice little condo outside of Bad News city limits, in the cut, because living with Jazzy or his mom was rough.

50 had Jazzy's legs in the air and his face between her thick thighs. He was eating her out as if he ain't eat all day.

"Shhhiitttt..." she moaned, about to cum again on his face. She bit the pillow while climaxing, to muffle her screams.

50 got from between her legs with a glazed face, making her laugh seeing her juices trickle down his chin.

Jazzy was ready to ride, so she didn't waste any time sitting on his pole. She rode him so good he nutted within seconds while she kissed his lips.

She wanted to feel him from the back, so she bent over in front of him, showing her phat, nicely shaved coochie with her juices dripping out.

50 had enough energy to finish the job, so he entered her from behind. He loved the feeling of her tight warmness, because every time he fucked her, it felt like the first time.

"Ahhh, yesss, fuck me baby," she screamed while he worked his way all through her tunnel, hitting G-spot.

"I'm cummingggg..." she shouted at the top of her lungs.

When she came, she pushed him out of her. It was too much dick and her body went limp.

"I caught my second wind, now you wanna quit." 50 laid down, penis still hard.

"I'm trying, babe," she stated.

"You ain't do shit all day except shop," he told her, checking his call log.

"Whatever."

"When we gonna get my body done, baby? You told me last month," she cried.

"I've been having so much going on," he told her, being honest.

"Oh yeah? Boy, please, tell that to a bitch who don't know."

"You are a pain in my ass," he replied.

"I know, that's why you love me," she said.

"Yeap, now what's happenin' wit' a round two?" he said, sliding his finger into her wetness.

***

Stafford, VA

Ja and Racks sat in the blue Crown Vic behind the tint, watching Capo and his soldiers sell drugs and hang out.

"You sure that's him, cuz?" Ja asked his cousin, who was staring out the passenger side window.

"Yeah, bruh, that's his bitch ass. I should have killed that hoe ass nigga," Racks stated, with an AK-47 in his lap.

"You should have killed him, then we wouldn't be here right now," Ja said, making sense.

"They caught me slippin'," Racks admitted.

"Well, it's your time to shine now," Ja said, hopping out with his Mack 10 submachine gun.

Capo was posted up on a block in front of the project build he grew up in.

"Aye, bro, you tryna slide to Bad News tonight? I gotta go get Pookie. This nigga on one," Capo told his little cousin, JuJu.

"Hell nah, folk, I ain't fucking with that wild, crazy nigga. You remember last time he was here he killed that old nigga for looking at him crazy," JuJu said, smoking a blunt of loud.

"Nah, he said the old nigga flipped him the middle finger." Capo laughed because he knew how burned out his boy was.

"That was somebody grandpop, dawg," JuJu replied as he saw two niggas creeping from across the street.

"It's a hit!" JuJu yelled as everybody pulled out their guns.

Tat

Tat

Tat

Tat

Tat

Tat

JuJu caught three to the chest, spinning him around like a DJ on the turntables.

Capo fired back, almost taking off Ja's head.

Bloc

Bloc

Bloc

Bloc

Capo went bullet for bullet after Racks took out two of his men.

"Fuck!" Capo yelled, seeing four soldiers come from behind his build with choppers.

Tat-tat-tat-tat-tatt-tat-tat-tat...

Ja and Rack only had fifty-round clips, and they knew this fight would have to be continued, just not right now.

"Come on, cuz," Ja told Racks, getting off the floor, creeping back to the car, praying none of the bullets hit them.

Capo saw Ja and Racks run off, then he saw JuJu's dead body and closed his eyes.

Capo and his young boys ran through the projects to the back to hide their weapons before the police arrived and searched the area.

Chapter 11

Bad News, VA

Pookie dropped off his girl, TeeTee, at work. He met her a while back in a mental inpatient treatment center, and the lovebirds had been boo'd up ever since.

TeeTee was slim and high yellow, with goldish hair and a pretty face. She suffered from a lot of depression, which led her to a couple of suicide attempts.

She and Pookie recently moved in together in a nice apartment. They had their relationship moments, but overall, it was more good than bad. Two crazy people together was always a struggle.

Don was hitting Pookie off with sixty keys every trip, and he was breaking the birds down into grams.

With his own projects on the Northside, he was feeding his whole hood.

Pookie had to pick up some money from his boy, JD, who was moving weight for Pookie.

He parked in the back lot near the basketball court and project pool. It was a nice hot day, so Pookie got out the car to go shoot some basketball real quick before JD came out.

Pookie didn't even see Melly creep out from behind the dumpster with an AK-47.

Tat-Tat-Tat-Tat-Tat-Tat…

As soon as Pookie heard the first shot, he dropped to the ground on one knee, grabbing his gun, spinning around firing shots toward Melly.

"Motherfucker!" Melly yelled, hidden behind the dumpster trying to avoid being shot.

Melly thought he had Pookie, but he was moving like he was some type of assassin.

Tat-Tat-Tat-Tat-Tat-Tat-Tat-Tat-Tat-Tat...
When he saw Pookie do a front flip over the front hood of a car to duck bullets, he knew Pookie was on some other shit.
Boc, Boc, Boc, Boc...
Tat-Tat-Tat-Tat-Tat-Tat...
Both shooters were moving like pros, ducking, dodging, and shooting.

The gunfire lasted another two minutes before it stopped, and Melly ran off just in time to see JD and six other men running toward the opposite direction with guns.

Pookie saw Melly was long gone, and he laughed because he just reloaded and was getting warmed up.

***

Manassas, VA

Homo's girl, Unique, was a tall, sexy, petite, dark choco-late woman with a career as an up-and-coming attorney with one of the biggest law firms in VA.

It was 7 p.m. and Unique was walking out of the attorney's office on her way to her car.

Focused on texting Homo, she didn't see the green Tahoe truck coming from the side and smashing into her.

The driver of the truck got out and saw Unique laid out on the floor, trying to move. The man tossed a pillowcase over her head and a zip tie around her neck.

The man tossed her into the truck before pulling off.

***

Bad News, VA

Don took the pillow case off her head.

"Please, I've done nothing wrong… You have the wrong person. I am a lawyer!" she shouted.

"Bitch, you're a lawyer assistant, stop lying," Capo said, laughing, sitting across from her in the old recreation center that was behind their projects.

Unique had been with Homo for a couple of months and knew nothing about his lifestyle. He told her he owed a barber shop, which he did.

"Tell me everything you know about Homo," Don said, pulling a chair up in front of her.

"I don't know a Homo."

"This bitch lying." Capo jumped up, ready to put hands and feet on a bitch.

"Chill, dawg," Don told his boy.

"Who are you talking about, my boyfriend, Marcus Clark?" She didn't know Homo by his street name.

"Yesss, I'm trying to have patience. Please, tell me everything you know about your boyfriend," Don asked calmly.

"He got two houses, one in Manassas and one in Virginia Beach. I know about a barbershop he has Downtown Manassas, but that's all I know. I don't even know his age, birth date, or nothing," she stated, feeling like a whore because she knew nothing about him except he had good charm.

"I'ma take your word for it, shawdy," Don said, standing up as if he was about to leave, but he was going to get a couple of heavy-duty garbage bags.

"Can I go now?" she cried, making Capo laugh because he knew the answer was that they were sending Homo a welcome home gift.

"How do you want to do this?" Don asked Capo, passing him a toolkit as Pookie walked in.

"What I miss, bruh?" Pookie asked.

"You're just in time." Capo passed Pookie the tool kit, seeing him smile.

"Chop her in half and let's drop her off at our boy's doorstep," Don stated as Unique cried.

***

Manassas, VA
Two Days Later

Homo pulled into his driveway, hoping Unique was home because he ain't seen her in two days.

Homo walked up to his doorstep to see a black garbage with a note that read Merry Xmas.

When Homo opened the bag, he saw half of Unique's body covered in blood. He ran back to his car, driving far away because the cops knew where he lived. He knew Unique told them everything she knew.

Chapter 12

Bad News, VA

Tank Brim just dropped 50 off in the hood, and he was starving, so he was on his way to Ihop to eat breakfast.

Tank Brim and 50 had North Bad News on lock. They had formed a little crew in the town.

Word was Ja and Racks dropped a couple of bands on their head, so Tank Brim rode around with two guns on the seat and an SK in the trunk.

In a couple of hours, Tank Brim had to pick up his little brother from school, then he had to get up with 50.

They needed a plug quickly. Tank Brim tried to tell 50 to holler at CL since he had half of VA under his belt.

Pulling into the lot, he saw Capo coming out with a plastic cup in his hand full of orange juice.

Tank Brim disliked anybody who dealt with Don, and Capo was Don's right-hand man. The whole city knew that.

Getting out of the car, both men stared each other down.

"You see something you like, dawg?" Capo shouted.

"I should be asking you that, bruh. You all on my dick, hoe nigga," Tank Brim shot, seeing Capo's face screw up.

"Who the fuck you talking to, bitch nigga? I'll kill you out cha." Capo rushed toward Tank Brim.

When Tank Brim pulled out a 4, Capo went for his.

Bloc, Bloc, Bloc...

Boc, Boc...

Bloc, Bloc, Bloc, Bloc...

The men were ducking behind cars, shooting back and forth at each other.

"I'ma catch you, nigga." Capo got in his car, burning rubber out the lot. He ain't have time for the back and forth shooting game early this morning.

Tank Brim saw civilians taking pictures of him before he climbed back in his car, leaving before the police made their way down there.

Anytime gunfire accrued, white people were known for calling the police on niggas, and Tank Brim didn't feel like going back to jail. He loved his freedom.

***

Hampton, VA

"Bruh, I'm finna kill that hoe ass nigga when I see him. Who does he think he is dealing with? He must not know who I am." Capo walked in circles in the background of Don's mansion.

Don sat in a chair sipping on lean, paying Capo no mind as he thought about what Tank Brim and 50 had up their sleeves.

A few weeks ago, Don heard some niggas had money on his little brother's head, but Don had his own issues to worry about.

"Sit down, please, you're driving me crazy, bruh. You not gonna do shit until I figure this shit out, because something ain't right. I feel like I'm missing something," Don said, looking into the sky-blue clouds.

"Oh, you on some brotherly love shit (laugh). When they start coming for your head, I want you to say the same sucker shit you just told me." Capo walked off, on fire, ready to kill something.

Don sat there thinking why was 50 acting different, then it hit him like a ton of bricks.

"Oh, shit…" Don shouted to himself.

***

Norfolk, VA

Shay had her legs over her boyfriend's shoulders while he went deep in her, riding into her wetness.

"Ohhhh, Melly, oh fuck!" she screamed, feeling him in her core.

Melly listened to the loud sound of his penis entering her gushiness. He loved the way her walls squeezed his pole. He couldn't control himself.

"I'm cumminggg, baby…" he moaned as she grabbed his ass cheeks, forcing him deeper into her little kitty.

"Cumm in me, daddy," she begged, looking into his eyes. Shay loved the way Melly fucked her and made love to her. It was so passionate.

"I wanna try this thing, baby, but take it slow, baby," Shay said, passing him the KY Jelly she brought today for this special event.

"You sure, baby?"

"Yes… Now come on before I change my mind," she said, bending over on the king-size bed in Melly's apartment on the outskirts of Norfolk.

Melly placed the KY on his dick and placed some in her tiny brown hole. He slowly placed the tip of his pipe in her, making her scoot up.

"Shhitt…" she moaned as he gripped her petite waist and slowly went a little deeper while rubbing her long clit.

"Uhhhgggg, Melly!" she screamed, feeling him halfway in her back door.

Once she got relaxed, he was fucking the shit out her ass, stretching her out, and Shay was loving it.

After the love making, Melly had some business to attend to with CL, while Shay went to sleep thinking about marriage.

Chapter 13

Richmond, VA

The new casino in the city of Richmond was full this weekend for the NBA All-Star Game they were having in VA.

Tonight was Ja's birthday, and he was having the time of his life in the casino with a three-man crew and six women he brought out to have fun with him.

Racks left two hours ago to head back to Norfolk, Virginia so he could take care of some business.

Ja was at the black jack table losing money back to back while drinking Remy Martin on ice.

"I quit, fuck that shit. I just lost 60 fucking thousand dollars." Ja got up from the table.

"Let's go have sex upstairs in the jacuzzi," a pretty brown-skin chick with a fake ass and titties said, in a tight red dress.

Ja looked at her body and took a sip of his drink, ready to take the young woman up on her offer.

"Let's get outta here, shawdy, and that pussy better be tight," Ja whispered into her ear, smelling her strong perfume.

"I got that snap, daddy. You gonna need an hour to loosen me up," she shot back, following him and his crew upstairs.

Ja and his crew all stayed on the sixth floor in different rooms.

When they got off the elevator, everybody was laughing because one of the women threw up in the elevator because she couldn't hold liquor.

Everybody was so caught up in their sex plans, nobody saw the two masked men come out the stairwell door.

Boc...

Boc...

Boc...
Boc...
Boc...

Two of Ja's goons got hit, but Ja was quick on his feet as he used two women as shields while shooting between them.

Bloc...
Bloc...
Bloc...
Bloc...

Capo hid on the side of a room door as Lil' PJ did the same. Capo popped out shooting, hitting two females, seeing Ja run out the other stairwell.

Lil' PJ killed the rest of Ja's goons, except the women, who snuck inside one of the rooms while eight bodies laid in the hallway.

"Shit, he gone." Capo started running out the staircase with Lil' PJ, hoping to catch Ja outside.

***

Hampton, VA

Don was driving to a chick named Debra's crib he met last week. She told him to come over for dinner so they could get to know each other a little better in person.

Don entered the nice suburb area, only to see police lights flashing in his rearview mirror.

"What the fuck?" Don mumbled, pulling over at the beginning of a dead-end block where Debra told him she lived.

The young, white rookie cop got out of the car and walked to the new white Maybach.

"Nice car, but I need your license and registration, sir," the cop asked.

"Sure, but why are you pulling me over?" Don asked.

"Come on now, you're riding a new year Maybach in a suburban area," the cop said.

Don laughed and got his license and registration, but while he was passing the cop his license, he saw a shadow appear from the side of the house. Homo's face.

Shots went off, shattering Don's car windows, hitting the officer seven times, killing the cop.

Don's license and registration fell in his lap as the shooter was approaching the car at a fast pace. Don placed the car in reverse and ducked the rain of bullets.

Luckily, Don got a good look at Homo's face. Don knew that Debra tried to set him up. He felt like shit, but he was lucky to have made it out.

***

Tyson Corner Mall, VA

Racks was out picking up new outfits from some high-end designer stores.

With so much money flowing day-to-day, Racks just wanted to trick on women and blow money in clubs.

The only thing on his mind right now was figuring out who they were beefing with, because it seemed to him everybody was coming for their heads.

When he walked out the Gucci store, he saw a bad, thick Spanish bitch with a fat ass bustin' out her jeans.

Racks tapped her on the shoulder. Seeing her face up close, he had to have her.

"I don't mean to bother you, shorty, but I'm Racks, and I'm trying to get to know you," he said, making her burst out laughing.

Racks saw her laughing in his face, and he got upset.

"I'm good, nigga, I got a man," Jazzy told him, walking off.

Racks grabbed her arm.

"Bitch, who the fuck you talking to!" Racks yelled in front of everybody.

"Get the fuck off me!" Jazzy shouted, snatching her arm back.

Racks slapped her in her face in front of everybody.

"You fuck nigga, you gonna slap a chick! "Jazzy yelled, holding her burning face.

Racks walked off laughing.

Chapter 14

Norfolk, VA

Today, Cookie's daughter had a half day at school, so she took her daughter to the park near their home.

Cookie was a sexy chocolate woman with exotic features and a nice body she got from climbing stripper poles most of her life.

She was CL's baby mother number three. Even though they went their separate ways, CL still took care of her daughter and Cookie.

Since having a child, Cookie quit the club scene and now she started her own clothing store online, which was doing good.

Checking her watch, she saw it was time to go because CL was coming to get his daughter in 30 minutes.

"Baby, come on, let's go, your father should be on his way!" Cookie yelled at her daughter who was on the park slide with two other little girls.

Cookie and her daughter walked up the block to the house.

A young man was walking toward them on his way to the park. Cookie saw something scary in his eyes, which made her grab her daughter's hand.

"Do you know where the park is?" the man asked them, stopping in front of them, as if he was blocking their view.

"Yes, up the street... excuse me." Cookie tried to ease by the man, but when she saw him pull out a gun, she slid in front of her daughter.

"Sorry it's gotta be like this," Pookie whispered.

"Mommy, what is he doing? Mommy..." She hid behind her mom's leg, watching Pookie.

"Close your eyes, baby," Cookie told her, knowing this was karma from all her dirt done in her life.

Bloc, Bloc...

Pookie put two holes in her head. When Cookie's body fell on the curb, Pookie looked at her daughter's saddened eyes.

"It's Sunday, so I'mma let you live, go home," Pookie told the little girl before walking off.

***

Forty Minutes Later

CL drove up the street to see yellow caution tape everywhere, and police were directing drivers the other way until they figured out what happened.

"Officer, my daughter and baby mother live a couple of houses up. Can I park and go get them?" CL asked, pulling the windows down.

"Sorry, sir, we got a homicide here. It's crazy you say you have a girl, because a black woman was just killed, and her daughter told us they were waiting for her father to come pick them up."

Hearing this, CL jumped out of the car to see his daughter with two cops. Tears filled his eyes because he was glad his daughter was still alive.

***

Sux Prison, VA

Rich walked in the visit room with his smooth demeanor, to see Don sitting there talking to himself.

"I was starting to think talking to yourself was a jail thing, but I guess not," Rich stated, sitting down smiling.

"You got jokes, I see... I was just trying to figure some shit out. This fuck nigga, Homo, really starting to get on my fucking nerves, for real, dog," Don stated as Rich just listened.

One thing Don liked about his pops was he was a good listener and he understood the streets.

Don didn't know how his pop still had keys all over VA and he been down for years now. He respected his grind.

"Have patience, son. Homo is a killer under pressure. You know how to trap a bear?" Rich asked, leaning back in his chair.

"Nah, bruh, tell me."

"Feed him..." Rich stated, hoping he ain't go over Don's head just now.

"How you feed him?"

"When a bear smells fear, he will get aroused and so thirsty that he will lose everything. To get blood, you have to give it. So, who can you use as bait until you're able to strike?" Rich told him.

"I got you," Don said.

"I have good news for you. I got you a plug, and he wants to meet you soon, but I want to make sure you are ready." Rich saw his son smile.

"Wow, that's what's up." Don was more than excited because he was running low on dope and dog food was moving so fast in Bad News. If a dealer couldn't stay consistent, then he was exed out.

"Just give me a few weeks to set up everything, kid, and we off to the races. You got a bright future, just be a thinker," Rich told him.

***
Stafford, VA
1 week later

CL and his cousin, Ja, were at a movie theater parking lot talking about family members and the old times.

"I'm sorry about what happened to your daughter's mother, cuz, but we gon' get them niggas. Me and Racks on it, bruh. They almost killed me in the casino."

"Them niggas a problem, and we gotta get them out the way. I got Melly on the team," CL said.

"Melly a soldier. I heard Homo back. I hate that nigga. I hope they kill him before I do," Ja said, because he and Homo had beef for years after Homo killed Ja's best friend and shot Ja. The two men talked a little more about Don and plotting ways to take his circle down.

Chapter 15

Manassas, VA

Busta and Peanut were opening the keys on the table in the trap, weighing the raw coke the boss Melly just brought them so they could distribute it to their hood.

"Bruh, we ain't never have this much shit," Busta said, placing piles of coke on the scale.

"This twenty birds, bruh. I'm glad we can say we finally made it, because I was sick of doing hand to hand, you feel me, bruh," Peanut shot back before taking a hit of coke on the table with a rolled-up dollar bill.

"You need to quit that shit, dawg. You heard what Melly said. If he finds out we using, he ain't fucking with us, shawdy," Busta told his cousin, who had a vicious coke problem.

Busta was more of the hustler and Peanut was the shooter, but Busta was trying to put his cousin on to some money.

"Fuck Melly, that nigga been out the hood for a while now, bruh. We should rob this fuck nigga," Peanut suggested.

"Yo, bruh, that ain't no real nigga shit. We was just down bad on our last gram and bruh just put us on. Who do you know doing that nowadays, especially for us?" Busta said, trying to prove a point to his cousin, who had a shady way of thinking.

Busta ain't even trust his own cousin because he knew the first chance Peanut got, he was gonna double-cross him.

"Ight, blood, I feel you," Peanut said, checking his watch as if he had to go somewhere.

BOOM...

Two gunmen rushed in the trap with assault rifles.

"Y'all late," Peanut said, smiling, looking at Busta's facial expression.

"Nigga, bag all that shit up, yo, so we can get the fuck outta here," Tank Brim told his homie he'd known for years.

Tank Brim and Peanut did time in jail together and always kept in touch. When Peanut called Tank Brim telling him he had a new plug named Melly and was about to take over, that's when Tank Brim came up with the idea to rob Melly. And knowing Peanut's greedy and grimy ways, he was down.

"Sorry, cuz, but I gotta get it how I live," Peanut said, while placing all the bricks in a duffle bag, smiling.

"Fuck you, dog ass nigga," Busta shouted.

"Oh yeah, I bet that's why I been fucking your baby mother since last year. I love that shit she do when she riding a nigga." Peanut laughed while passing the bag to 50 and Tank Brim.

Peanut pulled out his gun and fired seven bullets into his cousin's chest. Peanut was always jealous of Busta since they were kids, because he always did better than him.

"Let's slide," Peanut said, but 50 and Tank Brim didn't move a bone.

"Nah, bruh, sometimes you gotta open your eyes before it's too late…" Tank Brim stated before pulling the trigger.

Bloc…

Bloc…

Bloc…

Bloc…

Tank Brim and 50 left the trap with a bag full of bricks, laughing at how thirsty Peanut was to set up his own blood.

***

Bad News, VA

Capo and Pookie sat in a Dodge truck watching the nice house on the outskirts of Bad News.

Capo was so busy texting his new joint, he wasn't paying attention to Racks' crib where he laid his head.

"I think we should go up there," Pookie said, focusing on the mission while Capo was doing whatever he was doing.

"What!!!!" Capo said, not hearing a word he said and not caring. Capo hated going on missions with other people. Pookie was his man, but sometimes he would be on some weird shit.

"Racks ain't coming here, it's already 2 a.m., dawg," Pookie made a point.

"I guess you might be right, but how do you want to get in, the front or back?" Capo asked.

"Back," Pookie said, putting on his ski mask and grabbing his pistol.

"Cool, folk, I'm wit dat." Capo got out and walked up the street to Racks' crib, creeping through the back yard.

"Shhhhhh… It's a dog in the corner," Capo told Pookie, seeing a big Pitbull sleeping next to a tree.

Capo feared dogs. He prayed the dog wouldn't wake up as he played with the back door locks until it opened, thanks to his locksmith tools.

The back door was inside of a laundry room, and that door led to the kitchen, where they heard footsteps.

Capo and Pookie looked at each other, giving each other a head nod.

They pushed the door open, running into the kitchen to see a nigga in booty shorts and a half shirt, showing his lower stomach.

"Oh my god," the man screamed, trying to figure out what was going on.

"I told you this the wrong house," Pookie told Capo, trying not to look at the gay nigga who had long hair and small, fake titties.

"You Racks' brother? Where is he?" Capo asked, disgusted.

"Brother… Racks is my boyfriend, he has been my man since the fourth grade. I got the ring and the house. Them little bitches he be fucking all for show, trust me. He loves him some man butt," Racks' boyfriend said, snapping his neck with no shame.

Pookie and Capo's stomachs flipped. They wished they would have never come inside.

Not trying to hear any more, both men filled his body with bullets before leaving out the back.

Capo hated undercover bisexual niggas like Racks, because he knew niggas like that were running around fucking bad bitches and spreading viruses.

Chapter 16

Richmond, VA
Two Weeks Later

Don pulled up at a small water front surrounded by recently built condos.

Today, Don was meeting the plug his dad, Rich, was hooking him up with. Rich told Don that Turky was a big-time heroin supplier in VA and West VA.

Don was excited about getting a new connect because money was coming fast and he was running outta bricks.

His crew was doing numbers. Even Pookie's crazy ass had a team moving weight out of a project in the north sections of Bad News.

An all-white Bentley SUV pulled up next to his Mercedes.

Don saw a black male in his early 30s hop out wearing jewelry and Versace. Don couldn't help but laugh because Turky was wearing more jewelry than Slick Rick.

"You Don?" Turkey asked in a deep voice, approaching Don, extending his hand.

"Yeah, that's me. Thanks for coming out. I'm sure you're a busy man." Don moved over so Turky could sit down on the bench.

"Anything for Rich, that's family, bruh. I'll do anything for him, but I hear you doing your thing out there in Bad News." Turkey crossed his leg, looking at the birds flying in packs around the water.

"I'm doing fair, but I can always do better," Don replied.

"That's why I'm here. I'ma make you a lot of money. I did my research on you, bruh, and I know you have demonstrated integrity in your personal affairs. Since your name been ringing in Bad News, I like what I been hearing," Turky stated.

"Damn, you must be connected." Don felt like he was slipping because if Turky had been watching him, he wondered who else.

"You can say that, but how many keys can you work with? Because I don't do anything under 500 a trip. My men move only after midnight, and you will need a storage in your city of choice where you would like the dope delivered," Turky told him.

"I was thinking about 250 keys on my first trip," Don said.

Turky didn't say a word as he thought about what Don just said, because he didn't do anything under 500, but Rich was like a brother to him.

"Look, I'm only gonna do this shit one time, but next time it's 500 keys or better," Turky said firmly.

"Ok, deal," Don said, smiling, extending his hand out to Turky.

***

Bad News, VA
One Week Later

Ms. Rivera was bent over as Capo had his hands on her thick hips and slid his erection in her tight wetness.

While he fucked her doggy-style, she pushed her ass back into him, letting out a low moan.

Capo and Ms. Rivera went on two dates, but tonight she wanted to break him off some good love.

They became a couple last week, but she was holding out on the pussy and Capo now knew why. Her shit was like an ocean how wet she got.

74

"Uggghhhhh, I'm cumming…" she screamed, cumming on his rod.

Capo continued to fuck her, slap her ass, and pull her hair and shoulders back, diving deeper into her moist sex box.

After Capo nutted, he was drained. He couldn't go any more.

"How was it, baby?" she said, gasping for breath because they'd been having sex for 2 ½ hours with a one-minute break.

"Don't be surprised if you see me following you around town," Capo said, making her laugh hard.

"Oh, shut up." She tossed a pillow at him. She really liked Capo. He was cute, a real gentleman, and a thug.

"I love it, baby." Capo kissed her on her soft, juicy lips then made his way down south to her peach and ate her out.

***

North Bad News, VA

Purp was in the last house on the dead end of the back of James Allen Projects where he was from.

The dog food he and his guys were selling for Pookie had the hood going and the fiends going crazy.

Five of Purp's homies were all waiting on some women to come through. They had weed and liquor for them.

The doorbell rang, taking the men out of their thoughts as they were playing cards for big money.

"Yo, Kevin, you got the fat bitch, bruh. I fucked her stank pussy ass last time," Purp said on his way to open the door.

When Purp opened the door, his smile turned into a frown before six slugs hit his heart.

Four gunmen ran in the crib, shooting the crib with AK-47s and Dracos. When everybody was dead, Ja and Racks walked out with their two-man crew.

Ja and Racks wanted Pookie and Capo's blood. Racks ain't tell Ja they killed his boyfriend. Instead, he told him the ops killed his girlfriend, because nobody knew he was bisexual except a few niggas he was in jail with, because he had a boyfriend in prison.

Chapter 17

Dale City, VA

Twin was posted up in the hood down the street from Potomac Mall, getting money with his man, Marva, he knew since he was a little kid.

Roc was in Norfolk trapping, because they thought it would be better to sell drugs in different areas.

"Yo, bruh, this work is fire. I'm moving a key a day alone in just this one block, dawg," Marva said, looking up the dark block for any fiens, because at night time they came out like zombies.

"We got the best dog food in VA," Twin started seriously, rolling a blunt of loud.

"What's up with them Woodbridge niggas, you still be fucking wit' dem?" Marva didn't deal in many hoods in VA, other than Dale City.

"Bruh, them niggas ain't worried about you. That beef been dead, but Rock be out there from time to time."

"I don't know why. That shit ghost town, ain't no money out there, folk," Marva said, while two dopeheads approached him with $100 apiece.

Marva served both of the dope heads, giving them one bundle apiece, and they ran off smiling.

"That shit had four fiends OD'd in two days, bro. Y'all got to cut this shit more. Y'all niggas out here killing good things and all the big spenders." Marva laughed, but he was serious.

"They'll be aight." Twin just so happened to look up the street to see a man running toward them with a weapon.

Bloc...

Bloc...

Bloc...
Bloc...
Bloc...

Twin got low, crawling on the side of a Benz truck. He saw Marva ain't move fast enough, because his body was on the ground bleeding out his neck.

Bloc...
Bloc...
Bloc...

Twin fired back, stopping the man in his tracks.

Pookie saw Twin fire back, and he hid on the side of a building trying not to get hit.

He thought Marva was Twin from a distance, but up close, he knew he fucked up.

Pookie and Twin were going shot-for-shot until both men's guns were empty. Pookie had another clip in his back pocket, but by the time he reloaded, he saw Twin running down the street.

Pookie let off ten rounds and two hit Twin in his ass, but he limped until he made it into one of the buildings.

"Shit..." Pookie left the scene, knowing he would relive this moment again one day.

***

Bad News, VA

Jazzy was with her friend, Missy, driving 50's car on her way to go out clubbing in Richmond.

"I heard this club be so lit, girl. I swear I'ma find me a nigga tonight, I swear," Missy said, looking at herself in the mirror.

Both women looked amazing in dresses and heels, ready to go out and enjoy the night. Two of their homegirls were already in Richmond waiting for them.

Jazzy stopped the car at a red light near a gas station. Jazzy saw a black BMW with tints pull up on the passenger side.

When the BMW windows rolled down, fire and lights were all Jazzy saw before Missy's head blew off.

Jazzy hit the gas, racing off to get away from the BMW while crying for her girl's death.

Racks spun the block then went to change cars, because he knew the police would soon be looking for a BMW.

Racks recently found out 50 had a girlfriend, and it was the same girl he slapped fire out of at the mall a few weeks back.

Ja and Racks were on the hunt for 50 and Tank Brim, and Racks wasn't gonna stop. But his main worry was Capo and Lil' PJ, because they knew his secret.

Romell Tukes

Chapter 18

Richmond, VA

CL was standing on his terrace thinking about what just happened two days ago when he was robbed.

CL had never been robbed in his life. People feared him enough not to rob him or even think of crossing that line.

There was no doubt in his mind that New York nigga robbed him. CL knew up north slang, and the nigga who robbed him was from New York without question.

In VA, a lot of New York cats came down to get money, but a lot of them got sent back in body bags.

He was staring at the sky, thinking how bad it made him look. CL was ready to drop a bag on the New York cat's hat.

CL was tripping about the money and was worried about who would find out he just robbed. The whole situation was so crazy that CL was ready to skip town for a while until his robber's head popped up.

***

Northeast, DC.

"I'm telling you, bruh, this is going to be big time, trust me. I knew KG ain't coming back and forth out here for nothing. This nigga be moving dem things in the hood, shawdy," 50 said, following the Audi three cars ahead of them.

"I don't know, bruh, but the fuck is this nigga taking us?" Tank Brim said, as they rode past a police station.

"Wherever he taking us, I know this will be our big break, dawg. I'm glad you found him, because I thought he moved to Atlanta," 50 stated, trying to keep up with the Audi without being seen.

"He was in da 'A,' bruh, they say he was down there getting big money," Tank Brim replied.

"I guess he's gonna make his move here, bruh, but we gotta use the silencers. There was a police station up the block," Don said, directing 50 to pull into a rundown, cheap motel.

"We're just here?" Tank Brim asked, seeing KG got out his car going into one of the rooms with a duffle bag.

"Yeap, where you got to go?" Don asked, parking at the end of the lot.

Five minutes later, they saw a pink McLaren Spyder pull up with a black truck behind it.

"That shit nice, bruh." Tank Brim stared at the person driving the car, but he couldn't get a good look.

When they saw a bad redbone bitch get out wearing a white dress and heels, their mouths dropped.

"Damnnnnn…" was all they could say, seeing her catwalk in the hotel room. They saw two big, stocky niggas hop out with two duffle bags and place them in the back of KG's car.

KG opened the hotel door for his plug, Gotti's sister, who had the DC drug trade on lock with dope. She was young, beautiful, and deadly.

"KG, how's everything?" she asked, smiling.

"I'm good, thanks for meeting me. This is all of it." KG passed the duffle bags, trying hard not to look at her body or curves.

"Ok, good, no need for me to count, you always come right, but you going back to ATL? You was doing real good down there. I think VA holds people back from becoming a big success because it's too much snitching," she said, keeping it real with him.

"Atlanta is no better. Niggas is telling everywhere now," KG told her.

"You're right about that, but I gotta go. Your stuff is in the Audi. Be safe and always watch your surroundings," she said before leaving.

What she said went over KG's head. He was a little slower than most street hustlers.

"She's coming out," Don said, seeing Stephen come out, looking him in his eyes. "Damn, I think she just saw us!" Don shouted, trying to duck in his seat.

"You trippin', dawg, she pulled out the lot," Tank Brim said, seeing her and the truck roll out.

"I'm staying here and following you in the Audi. It's broad daylight, bruh, wear a ski mask," Don told Tank Brim, who laughed at him.

"Nigga, who I look like, the KKK?" Tank Brim hopped out the same time he saw KG come out the room.

KG popped his trunk to make sure everything was there and in place. The only thing he feared was getting pulled over.

There was no doubt in his mind that if he got pulled over, he was ratting on Stephen. He'd been wanting to fuck her since he met her in Atlanta, but she wasn't going for it.

KG was a pretty light-skin nigga, and he normally had any bitch he wanted, except her.

Closing the trunk, he went for his car door.

PSST...

PSST...

PSST...

"Ahhhhh... Fuck, niggga...ahh..." he screamed in pain. Tank Brim stood over him and shot him one more time in his skull, before taking the car, driving out the lot with a car full of bricks of dog food.

Romell Tukes

Chapter 19

Bad News, VA

Captain Cole was in his office on a phone call with the FBI director of VA.

"Ok, I am looking into it, sir. You have my word on that, sir, as soon as I get off the phone… Have a good day." Cap. Cole slammed the phone down.

He just got a call from the FBI saying there was a kid named Don they were about to build a case on, and they needed his help.

The FBI was faxing him a pic and resume of the agent he was going to be working with undercover.

Cap. Cole knew if he let this go down, he'd be in a cell in a prison with Don somewhere.

Don had Cap. Cole and his payroll for over a year now, and things were going sweet until now.

He heard the fax machine, so he went to get everything and called Don to meet him at the golf course.

Cap. Cole went golfing every Friday in Hampton, VA, then he would go fuck a hooker and head home to have a couple of drinks. He left his office in a rush.

***

Hampton, VA
An Hour Later

Don was driving the Bentley to see what the fuck Cap. Cole wanted, because he already had Lil' PJ deal with him last week. Don hated dealing with police on any level because he knew they would snake him and lock his ass up at any given second.

He knew Cap. Cole's greed was too high for him to turn on him. One thing Don could say was Cap. Cole was letting these people get away with everything.

Every once in a while, he would do a house and lock up some niggas on petty charges just to make shit look good.

Don pulled into the golf course parking lot to see Cap. Cole in a pair of Polo shorts and t-shirt, looking like a real classy white boy.

Don didn't know this, but he was the reason why Cap. Cole could afford to be in golf clubs, go on yacht trips, and enjoy the finer things in life.

"Don, nice car," Cap. Cole said, holding a folder in his hand.

"Thanks, but what's going on? My people already paid you," Don said, with a concerned look, because chilling with police wasn't his thing.

"We have a big fucking bump in our road." Cap. Cole handed him the folder. "The FBI told me they are about to build a case on you, and they want my help. This person will be going undercover. I'm sure you're a very smart kid and you know what needs to be done, because I'm not going to jail." Cap. Cole walked off to go play golf.

Don saw the photo, and his heart stopped. He couldn't believe whose face he was looking at. This just changed the game.

***

Norfolk, VA
Two Weeks Later

Don rented a small fishing boat to go fishing on this nice summer day.

Things were going good, money was coming, and his plug was blessing him. Today, he would arrange for another shipment of dope with Turky, who was on his way to go fishing with it.

Lately, Don had been hearing his little brother's name a lot in the city of Bad News. Word was, he had two traps doing good.

He saw Capo last night and told him to end his beef with 50's friend, Tank Brim, but he wasn't trying to hear it. Don wanted to speak to 50 to see what was going on.

When Turky pulled up, Don got his fishing equipment and waited on Turky, who wasn't wearing his jewelry but an old fisher hat.

"Fishing, I like this" Turky said, walking with Don to the boat.

The men drank a couple of beers as they sailed into the deep ocean.

"It's a perfect day for fishing, but I still ain't catch shit (laugh)," Turky said, holding his fishing pole in the water.

"You know what's crazy, whenever I fish, I always have the most trouble with the smallest fish," Don said, laughing.

"I can dig that, but how's business? You been copping heavy lately," Turkey said, knowing Don was a gold mine.

"I'm glad you mentioned it, because the feds are on my line and about to send an undercover cop at me," Don said.

"What! That's crazy why? You have to get to the bottom of this." He truly sounded upset.

"That's why we're here," Don said, training his gun on him, to see the shocked expression.

"Don, please, I'm an agent. You will go to prison for life if you kill me!" Turky screamed, fearing for his life, wishing he never took the case.

"Who sent you?"

"Rich contacted us with an offer to set up so we can build a case on you and your crew. There are so many bodies in Bad News because of you and your crew. We was gonna give your dad a time cut just to get y'all," Turky said.

"Rich set me up?"

"Yes, I'm sorry, but he's working for us. Who do you think got you all them keyz?"

"Y'all have a big, solid case on me?"

"No, not yet," Turky said before Don shot him in the head and tossed him in the ocean. Don was sick and couldn't believe what was going on.

Chapter 20

Manassas, VA

Melly's aunt, Jalees, just got caught up in a big drug raid by the local police in Georgetown south area.

Jalees was a coke head who stepped her game up to crack. She was in her mid forties and looking bad, but she still had a phat ass.

This was about to be her second time going to jail, and she couldn't do another bid in a dirty ass cell.

She waited in the interrogation room for a local detective to arrive, because she had a plan to use her get outta jail card today. She'd been holding her wild card for some time now.

"Jalees, I see you still out here up to no good. I thought you got clean," a white detective asked as he walked inside the room.

"I did get clean, this was a set up!" Jalees shouted.

"Oh, a set up? So that's how you got caught with a pipe in your mouth?" the detective stated.

"Shit happens, but I have some info that is better than anything you received all year. I just need to know I'm firna be walking out this bitch today," she said, snapping her neck and fingers.

"It depends on what you got for me, and if it's accurate, because a crackhead will say anything to get out of jail. I've seen it all," the detective said with a chuckle.

"This about a couple of murders, and one was my son," she said sadly, trying not to get emotional.

When she lost her son to the streets, she turned back to smoking crack.

Jalees now had the cop's full attention. He was ready to take note.

"Ok, I'm listening…" he said.

Jalees told him about three murders she saw Melly do, including when he killed her own first cousin because he stole some money from Melly.

After two hours of ratting, the detective had a solid case on Melly and all the homicides she told him about were on his caseload, so he was overwhelmed.

The detective made some calls to drop all of Jalees' recent charges, and she was able to walk free.

Jalees walked out the precinct smiling, thinking about her next hit. She was walking down the block on her way to the hood when a Lexus pulled up on the side of her.

"Aunty…" The windows rolled down.

When Jalees saw Melly, she thought she saw a ghost.

"Melly…?" she asked, dumbfounded.

"Get in," he said.

"I'm good, nephew, I'm just going down the block," she told him, sweating.

"I'm going the same way, get in," he told her, pushing the passenger door open for her.

She didn't want him to think no funny shit, so she went inside.

When Melly pulled off, he turned down the music, happy to see his aunt.

"I heard you got caught in a raid today," Melly said, keeping his eyes on the road.

"Me, nah, I was at home, nephew, ain't hear about that," she replied quickly.

"You just came out of the police station, didn't you?" asked Melly.

"Yeah, but it was for a bullshit warrant from years ago. A traffic warrant. But what's up with all the questions, ain't you happy to see your aunty?" she asked.

"No, not really, because I got a call today from one of the detectives who I have on the payroll. He was telling me my aunt was down in his station ratting on me about some murders." Melly pulled into a small alleyway behind a shopping center.

"That wasn't me." Jalees reached for the door handle, but the child lock was on.

"You dirty bitch." Melly took her head and banged it into the dashboard before pulling out his weapon.

"Melly, I'm sorry," she cried.

Melly shot her twice in the head and kicked her out the car.

***

Las Vegas, NV

Don, Pookie, Lil' PJ, and Capo were in a huge club on the third level VIP section with ten beautiful women, drinking and having fun.

The gang all thought it would be wise to get out of town for a week or two because too much was going on.

Bad News had been a kill zone for the last month. Since Don killed the FBI agent, the city had been under close watch. Luckily, the day Turky went to meet Don he wasn't wired because he was trying to side deal for himself.

Don was still fucked up that his own dad was trying to set him up to get a time cut.

Don had an idea to get Rich back that he was going to put in full effect as soon as he got back to the city. He knew Rich had too much shit on him, and that's what Don was scared of.

Little did Don know, Turky was doing a lot of side deals for himself, so the FBI didn't have anything on Don because

Turky had been supplying him with his own drugs he stole from kingpins.

Chapter 21

Hampton, VA

Spring was in VA for a couple of months to visit. She lived in Atlanta where she worked in computer marketing.

Spring was a beautiful, short, light-skin, petite woman with class, but she was also a true freak.

Racks was her brother, but the two fell out years ago because she caught Racks fucking her boyfriend at the time. She had no clue either one of them was gay. She never spoke to either of them again.

She was in her condo waiting on her date to come through. She wore a nice dress with heels and her long hair wrapped in a bun.

Her buzzer rang, so she went to answer it and saw Homo standing there in a Dior outfit.

The two went to school together. They had a close relationship, but they hadn't seen each other in 10 years. They surfaced on Facebook last month and they had been talking on-stop since.

"Damn, girl, you got thick," Homo told her, walking inside taking off his coat.

"Thank you, a bitch been eating really good. What's up with you though?" she asked.

"Same ole thing," Homo said, looking at her thighs as she crossed her legs.

"That's good, so you don't have nobody special you're dealing with? Since you are electric sliding in my DM and shit," Spring said, laughing.

"I been trying fuck you for years," he told her, pouring himself a glass of Patrón that sat on the table.

"Oh, wow, is that right? Tonight may be your lucky night. I'm horny and ready to get fucked," she told him, giving him a sexual look.

"What we waiting for?" he said, getting up.

"I thought you'd never ask," she replied, taking him to the back room.

They fucked like two wild jungle animals all night long until sunset brightened the bedroom.

Homo hated Racks and he knew Spring was his sister, so fucking her just made him gain a big laugh.

Homo and Racks were locked up in prison years ago.

Homo knew Racks was gay. He was a gay thug killing shit in the street, but Homo didn't respect that because he was a real live street nigga.

***

Norfolk, VA

Roc and Twin's mom were cleaning up Roc's new mini mansion he recently bought.

His mom saw a truck pull up in the front driveway on the living room cameras.

She knew Roc's friends came by all day, so she went to open the door.

When the door opened, she saw two men with guns pointed to her face.

"Take us to Roc's stash," 50 said, pointing his Glock 40 at her face.

"It's in the wine room downstairs. Take it all, please, and may the Lord be with you both," she said as Tank Brim ran downstairs as he forced her into the living room.

"Where is your son?" 50 asked.

"I know a smart young man like yourself will find him," she replied, sitting down.

"You got a smart mouth, old bitch," 50 said, looking behind him to see what was taking Tank Brim so long.

50 got the drop on Roc when he followed him home from the club one night.

When he turned around, he saw Roc's mom somehow slid a gun from under the couch.

Boc...

Boc...

50 ducked the bullets and fired two bullets into Roc's mom's head himself as his heart aced.

Tank Brim ran upstairs with a gun in his hand and a duffle bag in the other.

"Damn, bruh, you killed Grandma." Tank Brim laughed.

"Nigga, the old bitch tried to kill me," 50 said, walking out the house, shaking his head, not seeing the cameras above his head.

"Fuck her, shawdy." Tank Brim tossed the bag in the truck and pulled off.

***

Bad News, VA
Two Weeks Later

Don just got back in town last night and he was already in some good pussy.

He had Norway bent over, fucking her doggy-style for the last twelve minutes, throwing her big ass back on his dick.

Don felt himself about to cum, so he pulled out and shot his load in his hand.

"Why did you stop? I ain't get mine," Norway asked, looking back at him.

"My bad." Don went to wash his hands in the hotel sink, which had roaches in it crawling everywhere.

Norway was Melly's sister. She wasn't too cute, but she had a crazy body. She met Don an hour ago at a pizza shop, and that led to a dirty hotel room.

Don stepped into the bathroom with a gun in his hand, to see her face light up in fear.

Bloc…
Bloc…
Bloc…

Don got dressed and left the hotel room.

Chapter 22

Bad News, VA

50 just arrived at his brother K's gravesite with a bottle of D'Ussé for himself.

At least once a month, he would come visit and pour some liquor for his brother, because he always took care of him when he was younger and he always remembered that.

Since 50 had been robbing niggas and feeding his hood, everything around him seemed like a movie.

His life was going at a fast pace. He believed in karma but he also believed when it was his time, then it was his time.

Tank Brim was the only person he felt like he could trust and even with him, he felt as if he had to keep a close eye on him.

Things with Jazzy were going good. She was in New York with her sister doing some shopping.

50 looked at his brother's tombstone and shed a tear. Knowing the nigga who killed him was still out there made him hate himself more.

When he found out Don killed K, he was fucked in the head about that, because he couldn't push himself to kill his own blood.

In the back of his mind, he wondered what made Don do it. He asked himself that daily.

50 saw his mom, Ashley, text him, telling him to stop by the crib sometime today. 50 drank a couple more sips and poured the rest out on his brother's grave before he walked off.

50 was riding around with a Draco and a Glock 21 with thirty shots because he felt like he was the most wanted nigga in Bad News.

***

Richmond, VA
1 Week Later

Roc and Twin were at their mom's wake, looking at her dead body, in tears.

"Yo, I'ma kill them niggas," Twin told Roc as they both entered the small house.

"I can't believe this shit, bro," Roc said, pissed off, holding back his tears.

"I'm ready to ride on these niggas," Twin stated seriously.

"Na, chill bruh, we gonna play in the background on this day," Roc said.

"What, fuck that shit, nigga. Them niggas killed our mom and you out here acting like a scared bitch," Twin stated.

"Watch who you talking to, but just chill, bruh. We got them niggas on camera, so just chill. We gonna strike when the time is right," Roc said before climbing in his coupe.

"You do you and I'ma do me, bruh," Twin said, walking off.

***

Bad News, VA

Pastor Ryan just finished his Wednesday service with the elder women in the church.

Pastor Ryan stared at the Holy Bible, thinking about his time he served in the army, where he killed so many people he forgot most of them.

Every night he had nightmares about killing, and his wife was the only person who could calm him down.

"Hey, baby, what's going on, are you ready to go home?" his wife said, walking down the aisle in a black dress. She was a beautiful dark-skin woman with a nice smile and wide shape.

"Yes, I'm ready to start the car up," Pastor Ryan told his wife, smiling.

Pastor Ryan was grateful to have a beautiful wife and a happy life. When he got saved and gave his life to the Lord, he became devoted to the Lord.

He gave up his life of violence. He knew what his son was in the streets doing, and he prayed the Lord would save him.

***

Across Town

Don was driving in a stolen car on his way to pick up Capo so they could go put in some work.

He heard Homo was across town, over the bridge, at some bitch's house. He didn't want to miss this chance to catch Capo slipping.

Romell Tukes

Chapter 23

Woodbridge, VA

Tank Brim was waiting to pick up some money from his big cousin, Whitey, who was selling drugs to Tank Brim.

Whitey was Tank Brim's first cousin, but he was a shady nigga nobody trusted, not even his own family or mother.

Tank Brim knew Whitey was fucked up and down bad, so he took it upon himself to help him.

It'd been a couple of weeks since he heard from Whitey, so he was parked outside of his baby mother's crib.

Family or no family, Tank Brim didn't play when it came to his money or niggas stealing from him.

Seeing a Spanish woman with a little boy walking out the apartment building made him focus on their new outfits.

The women had a Chanel outfit and purse, and the little boy rocked a Gucci outfit.

Tank Brim watched the BMW pull off and hopped out with his gun in his back.

Whitey was in his crib with the lights off and curtains closed, staring out the window while texting someone.

Whitey knew Tank was coming sooner or later for his money from the brick he fronted him.

Getting the brick off was the easy part, but keeping the money was the hard part, especially with a woman who wanted to be spoiled.

Tank Brim was banging on his door about to break it down.

"Shit, man." Whitey just got up and went to open the door to face the music, because Tank wasn't going anywhere.

"Whitey, you're playing vicious games, nigga. Where the fuck my money at?" Tank Brim stepped inside the dark crib.

"Just give me a few days. I got you, bro, that's on every-thing I love. You know how I do!" Whitey shouted.

"You spend my money on that bitch?"

"Nah, I had bills, but I got you, nigga. You know me, dawg," he cried to Tank, who pulled out a gun.

Bloc...

Bloc...

Bloc...

Bloc...

Bloc...

"Fuck outta here, hoe ass nigga." Tank Brim killed him and walked out the apartment.

When he crossed the street, shots rang out from behind him.

Twin got a call from his boy, Whitey, saying Tank Brim was coming over his house. Whitey heard Twin had 50k on Tank Brim's head. He wanted that money, plus he already owed Tank Brim, so having him killed was a double plus.

Twin snuck out from the side of the building, letting off shots, trying to take off Tank Brim's fitted cap.

BOOM!

BOOM!

Tank Brim fired in Twin's direction while trying to take cover, but the Mack 10 submachine gun Twin was firing was hitting everything around Tank.

The shooting lasted a couple more minutes before Tank Brim hopped in his car, pulling off.

Tank Brim had a .357 with seven shots and he ran outta bullets, so sticking around was out the question.

***

Stafford, VA

Capo was riding around blasting Yo Gotti and Money-bagg Yo's new album in his old school sitting on big rims.

He was about to drive out to Virginia Beach for a car show he attended every year.

His youngsta, Dee, was in the passenger seat rolling up a blunt of weed, taking a sip of molly water, feeling like he was on another level.

Capo saw a red Porsche 911 pull up on the passenger side of him, rolling down his window.

Before Capo said anything, a bullet tore through the passenger door, hitting Dee in his side, killing him. Capo fired shots out his window at the Porsche, shooting recklessly in the busy street. Training his eyes on the fleeing vehicle, he was able to make out the identity of the guy in the passenger's seat.

Capo pulled over and left the body on the side of the road because he was already dead, and taking him to the hospital was a waste of time.

Seeing Racks' face boiled his blood. He swore to get him back, but first he had to park the old school because it was fucked up and filled with bullet holes.

Romell Tukes

Chapter 24

Bad News, VA

Homo waited for 50 to arrive in the back of the warehouse parking lot.

The past couple of days, Homo had been hearing 50's name heavy through the streets, and rumor had it that 50 had killed his guys.

Homo wanted to see what all the hype was about, because he never heard of 50 until now, but he knew he was a young nigga.

A Mercedes AMG CLA pulled up with bright HD lights, blinding the truck Homo was in.

50 turned off his lights, grabbing his pistol before exiting his car.

When Homo reached out to him through one of his little niggas, he told him to set up a meeting.

Homo's name was heavy in the city. He was like a God in certain areas, and even when he left his name was still ringing.

"You 50?" Homo asked.

"You Homo?" 50 replied back, making him laugh.

"I heard a lot about you, bruh. I just wanted to meet you and chop it up, dawg," Homo told him.

"That's what's up," 50 shot back, sizing him up, trying to figure out his agenda.

"What you got going on in these streets, you're trying to get some money?" Homo looked like he was already doing good if the car wasn't leased.

"I'm out here trying to get some money, but what you had in mind, dog?" 50 asked.

"I need you on my team, bro. I got the best keys up in the city, I just need a nigga like yourself out here with me trying to run it up," Homo stated seriously, hoping 50 would join his team so he could take over the streets.

"I checked this out, bruh. I'm fucking with you, but just stay loyal to me and I'll give you the same," 50 told him, seeing a smile appear on his face.

***

Arlington, Virginia
2 Weeks Later

Don was locked up in Arlington County Jail, where his mother, Ashley, worked. He was upset he got caught with a gun. The cop dropped the charges he was pressing on Don for smashing into his patrol car, but he knew it was an accident.

Don went to court yesterday and the judge denied his bail, saying he would jump bail.

With so much going on in the streets, Don up didn't have time to be sitting in jail looking stupid.

He was standing on the inside rear deck looking outside, thinking about freedom. Earlier, he called Lil' PJ and told him to hold it down, and Lil' PJ knew what that meant word for word.

"Your ass don't fucking listen," a female voice said, approaching him from behind, and he turned around to see his mom in a CO uniform.

"Mom, nice to see you too."

"I just came back from vacation to hear my son was in here. How do you think I feel?" Ashley acted upset.

"I'm sorry, but shit happens," he stated, because he knew his mom was street smart. She may have looked like a dumb, pretty blond, but that wasn't the case at all.

"You got a gun charge. Do you know how long they give out for that?" she asked with her hands on her hips.

"I got a paid lawyer," he replied.

"I bet you do, but I'll be back later. I'm bringing you food, a phone, and a knife," she said, walking out shaking her head, to do her rounds in the CO books and every unit.

Don took a deep breath, looking into the clouds and his own thoughts.

***

Hampton, Virginia

Pookie and Lil' PJ were in Roc and Twin's grandma's house. They had her hands and ankles tied, exposing her whole lower body.

Lil' PJ had a young boy from his projects with them. The youngin', Ghetto, was a hitter, but he wasn't all there mentally.

"So you don't have your grandkids' number? Alright, go ahead and kill that bitch," Lil' PJ told Ghetto, who was sniffing her ass like a dog. Even Pookie looked at Ghetto like he'd lost his mind.

Ghetto pulled his hardened penis out and ran it in the old lady's asshole, making her scream in pain as he forced himself inside of her until blood was on his dick with shit coating it. Ghetto used her own gown to clean off the mixture of liquid on his dick.

Ghetto fired five shots into her head.

"What, bro," Ghetto said, looking at both men strangely.

"Let's go." Lil' PJ created a monster he didn't even know yet. Ghetto was Lil' PJ's personal hitter, and he would do anything for Lil' PJ.

Romell Tukes

Chapter 25

Hampton, Virginia
Hours Later

Roc couldn't believe the news he'd just received from his grandpa. Hearing his grandma was raped and killed in the house he bought her crushed him.

He knew his opps were responsible for the gruesome murder. He was on his way to visit his family and comfort them, because his grandma was the backbone.

Twin's phone was off. He knew his brother was sick and he knew why. He didn't like how shit had been going lately.

The twins didn't understand what was up. They were alone since Bree disappeared, so they were going up against an army with a few men.

Roc had to come up with something, because he was taking too many losses in a short matter of time.

Pulling up to his grandpa's crib, he saw over 20 cars and family members crying and mourning.

***

Stafford, Virginia

Miss Rivera was leaving her second job, thinking about her baby, Capo. She couldn't wait to get home to their new place to tell him the good news.

She found out she was pregnant this morning, which was the best news she'd heard all month.

Last week, her mother died of a heart attack, so she'd been stressed about that, but luckily, Capo was right there supporting her.

Miss Rivera was far from slow. She knew what Capo was doing in the streets, but she never questioned him.

She respected Capo because he kept his affairs in the streets. He never brought his street problems into their home.

As she walked to her car, a commercial van was blocking her car in.

The driver of the van walked from across the parking lot, seeing she was trying to get out.

"Excuse me, is this your van, sir? I'm just trying to get out," Miss Rivera told him respectfully.

The man looked at her then pulled out a gun.

"I'm sorry. I'll leave, you can stay there." Miss Rivera tried to turn to leave.

Boc...

Boc...

Boc...

Boc...

Melly stood over her body, making sure she was dead, before waking to the van.

When he pulled off, he tossed the gun out the window when he got a couple of blocks away from the crime scene.

Melly was hunting Capo, Lil' PJ, and Pookie's love ones down since he couldn't find Don.

Melly thought Don was somewhere hidden, but he had no clue he was locked up for a gun charge.

This was hunting season for Melly, and with CL behind him, he felt untouchable.

***

Bad News, Virginia

Tank Brim walked into a trap house where his workers sold dope and crack for him and 50.

Business had been good lately, and they were starting to see big money since dealing with Homo.

Tank Brim didn't like the idea of dealing with Homo when they could continue getting it out the mud by robbing and killing.

Homo had a rep in the streets for being grimy and keeping snake niggas close to him.

Tank Brim knew of Razor and Gangsta before they got killed, but he thought Homo was a ghost.

He didn't like the idea, but 50 said it was a chess move for a future power move. Tank was always going to ride with 50, so he just kept his mouth closed and enjoyed the ride.

"She in the back, bro. I ain't know she was yours..." *Whack!!*

The unexpected blow dropped the man to the floor.

Tank Brim went into the back room to see his older sister, Cara, on the floor high off dog food. She was with a pretty, light-skin, skinny, model-type chick who had a bad dope habit at the age of 28.

He loved his sister, but he knew the dog food was kicking her ass. He tried to help her many times, but she kept relapsing.

She basically raised him until drugs took her over four years ago. After her son and husband got murdered, she turned to drugs.

"Come on, baby girl, I got you." Tank Brim lifted her up and carried her out of his trap house.

When his little cousin called him and told him he saw her with Dave going into his trap, he knew what was up.

Romell Tukes

Chapter 26

Sux 2 Prison, VA
Four Months Later

Don was sentenced to two-year bid in state prison for his gun charge. Before he left Arlington County Jail, his mom had one of her close friends hit Don off with some, plus she was feeling him.

Don lucked up and was shipped to the same prison his dad was at and where his girlfriend Nicole worked at.

It was yard time, and he was waiting outside to meet up with his pops, who was housed next door to him.

Turky disappeared before Don caught his gun charge, so he made sure he played it smooth with Rich.

Don understood most niggas always showed their hand before they could even put their plans into action.

When he saw Rich coming out his unit with his security, he laughed to himself.

"Let's spin this track. I been cooped up in that unit all day under them begging ass niggas," Rich said as he saw his goons were waiting on the basketball court for him like they were guarding the president.

When prisoners heard Rich's son was on the yard, everybody tried to extend their hand, but Don knew better than to take something from another prisoner.

"How do you like your unit?" Rich asked him as the sun beamed on his skin.

"It sucks over there. Niggas is broke and miserable," Don replied.

"I'll get you moved to my unit tomorrow. I got a big cell for you, so you'll be at peace," Rich stated.

"Okay, that's good. I'm with that, but what you been up to over there?" Don asked him, stepping over a pile of ants.

"I'm getting a lot of money and focused on getting out, son," Rich stated, picking up on Don's silence, as if something was wrong. "You good?"

"Yeah, man, I'm focused on a bag since I'm stuck in here with you," Don said, walking past the football field.

"I will set you out, but how many times did you meet with Turky before he was killed?" Rich asked, sounding concerned.

"Never, why you ask? I was supposed to meet him before he got killed, but I had to go out of town," Don replied.

"So, you telling me you never did any business with him?" Rich stopped on the track.

"No..."

"Shit..."

"Why, what happened?" Don asked.

"Nothing, just asking." Rich looked stressed. They walked the yard for 20 more minutes. When Don got back to the unit, some niggas were plotting on a new dude who came from the Bronx but was in Norfolk getting money. There was money on the kid's head, but Don liked how he moved.

When the niggas ran up in the New York cat's cell, Don came in and stabbed a couple of dudes, almost killing one, saving the Bronx kid.

***

Dale City, Virginia

Pookie was coming out of a Western Union store getting six money orders to send Don.

He knew Don was financially stable, but he still felt it was his position to hold his boy down at whatever cost.

Shit had been going smooth in Bad News. Lil' PJ took over the drug operation, but he needed a plug, so he was focused on that more so than anything else.

He saw a thick, sexy, brown-skin woman climb out a BMW truck in some tight jeans with her ass hanging out.

The two made eye contact, and it was over.

"Hey, chocolate...." the woman said, walking past him, going in Western Union.

Pookie continued to walk, then he stopped, thinking about the woman. There was something about her that made him turn around.

Since he was a kid, Pookie had always been the shy, quiet kid who kept to himself, and it was good to talk to women.

Pookie waited for the woman to come back out. He wasn't going to let her slide out without shooting his shot.

"You following me, handsome?" the woman said, counting a big wad of blue faces.

"If you want."

"Maybe I do," she replied.

"What's your name?" Pookie asked her.

"I'm Ivy, how about you?"

"Pookie," he said, seeing her laugh as she thought about the Pookie from the *New Jack City* movie.

"Pookie huh, cute." She smiled.

"Are you busy tonight?"

"No, not no more, daddy. Take my number and call me later. Where you from?" she asked as they exchanged numbers.

"Bad News."

"Oh, you too? That's good, I'm on my way back to the city right now. Look out for my call, Cat Daddy," she said, climbing in the BMW truck, blowing him kisses.

Pookie was gone. He'd never felt this way about a chick in his life.

Chapter 27

Bad News, VA

Cara was in the Benz sniffing dog food off a small mirror, feeling the dope tingle in her body.

Five minutes ago, she ran into her cousin, Twin, who she hadn't seen in years. When she saw his luxury car, she knew he was doing big things.

He told her to get in so he could take her for a ride. When he pulled out a few bags of dope, she rushed to sniff it.

Sniffing dope made her extra horny all the time.

"This shit is good, Twin. Where you get this from? Can you get some more?" she asked, talking fast, as she always did when she was high.

"I got you, but I'm trying to fuck your little ass," Twin admitted.

"Twin, we cousins. You on that nasty shit, we kin." Cara sounded disgusted that he would even say some nasty shit like that.

"I got 10 bags for you, baby girl. I just want some head, shawty," he said, pulling out the dope.

Her eyes widened in shock. Cara was down to her last $15, so he came right on time.

"Okay, I'ma suck your dick, but don't nut in my mouth," she said, licking her fat, crusty lips.

Twin pulled his dick out, and she started from the tip of his dick, making her way down to the base, deepthroating his whole pipe with ease.

"Shitttttttt…" Twin moaned while she went up and down, using her lips to massage his rod as she picked up the pace.

Twin couldn't last any longer. He grabbed her head, pushing her down on his dick until he shot his come down her throat, making her choke.

"What the fuck, Twin?" she said, wiping his dripping come from under her bottom lip.

"Maybe I got caught up in the moment," he said, reaching under his seat.

"That's shit tastes nasty," she said, seeing Twin lift up the pistol.

Boc...

Boc...

Boc...

Boc...

Twin was already parked next to a dumpster, so he grabbed Cara's dead body and tossed it in the dumpster before pulling off.

Twin wished he would have gotten some head from Cara years ago, because her dick sucking game was on point.

***

Stafford, Virginia

Capo was on his motorcycle speeding through the city, on his way to check on some of his traps.

Since Don was in jail, Capo and Lil' PJ had been taking over all drug operations and shit was good, but there was only one big problem.

The crew needed a plug, and the only one in the city who had work for sale was CL, and he was on their hit list. Capo had to come up with a plan, because shit was going too good for them to run dry on work.

Luckily, they still had enough work left to hold them down another month or so.

Capo stopped at a red light and looked to his left, to see Homo coming out of a fast-food spot, walking to a Lexus sedan parked a couple of feet away from a cop car.

"Fuck that," Capo said to himself, making a left, pulling into the lot.

Homo just copped some burgers and fries for himself, and he was on his way to meet his new young boy, 50.

Homo was self-grooming 50 into the game. He liked the lil' nigga. He was a good listener and soaked up the game.

A blue and white motorcycle pulled up into the lot driving real slow. Homo paid it no mind because the cops were sitting in the cop car eating lunch, so whoever it was, they weren't crazy.

Bloc...

Bloc...

Bloc...

Bloc...

Homo hit the floor after the first shot went off while bullets hit his Lexus and the cop car.

Homo pulled out his weapon and fired back at the nigga with his helmet on his bike.

Boom...

Boom...

Even the cops got out firing at both men.

Capo shot one of the officers in his face twice, killing him, while the other called backup, hiding under the car.

Homo and Capo were going at it for a couple more seconds until sirens could be heard.

Capo burned rubber on the bike, doing a 12 in the air racing off, knowing he just killed a cop and he let Homo get away.

Romell Tukes

Chapter 28

Bad New, VA

"Oooh my god, baby," Ivy moaned out as Pookie was deeply inside her sweet wet spot.

This was their second date, which turned into a freak fest as soon as she stepped foot in Pookie's crib.

Ivy's big hips were raised up off the bed while Pookie fucked missionary as she began to squirt harder.

He loved the tight feel of her pussy gripping his erotic rod. Pookie lifted her right up, going in deep as his pelvis slapped against the bottom of her ass.

"Shit, I'm cummmmming again!" she screamed, rubbing her sensitive clit while Pookie continued to put a mean assault on her pussy.

"Oh my god! Ssssssss...." Ivy was gasping for air after he finally nut inside of her.

Pookie smiled, seeing he had her gone in the head, but there was no denying her pussy was hitting. She had a mean grip game.

"Where the fuck you been at all my life?" she asked, laughing while her legs were shaking.

"I'm here now, so that's all that matters, baby," Pookie said, putting his pole in front of her lips. She slowly made love to his dick with her mouth until he came again...

Pookie then fucked her fat ass doggy-style for the rest of the night.

***

Woodbridge, Virginia

50 just left Homo's crib in Woodbridge in the hood. 50 put a quarter of a million dollars for his next re-up because his last shipment was done.

He and Homo had been building a close relationship over the past couple of weeks. Business was going good for him and Tank Brim, moving dog food into two areas.

Pulling into the gas station, he saw Jazzy calling him. He ain't been spending time with her like that lately because he'd been focused on getting money while staying alive in the streets.

Racks was behind the tints in the Impala, watching 50's every move since he left Bad News.

Racks recently found out Don's little brother was the new kid on the block whose name was ringing bells.

What shocked him was 50 meeting up with Homo, because Racks did his research on Don's crew and found out Homo was their number one enemy.

None of this made sense to him, but he tried not to overthink it.

When he saw Homo, chills went through his body because he hadn't seen him in years.

Racks and Homo were locked up together, and Homo was his first male lover. Homo showed him how to suck dick and take it from the back. He used to be Homo's personal sex slave. The two used to have rough sex in the cell every night on the low.

Everything was cool until Homo cut ties with him because he heard Racks was fucking some other niggas in the library bathroom of the prison.

Racks hadn't seen him since, so when he recently ran into him, old feelings came back. Racks knew he had to focus on 50 right now, though.

He grabbed a Glock 30 and got out of the car, seeing 50 walk into the store. Racks snuck into the store as if he was doing some shopping.

Looking in the mirror on the corner ceiling, he saw 50 buying a soda, not paying attention to anyone.

Racks crept around the corner with his gun out, but 50 was on point. His weapon was already drawn, waiting on him.

Bloc...

Bloc...

Bloc...

"Bitch ass nigga!" Racks shouted, almost getting hit by one of 50's bullets.

Boc...

Boc...

Boc...

Racks shot out the glass windows where the sounds were.

50 dashed into the front of the store, firing a couple of shots at Racks to hold him down while he made his getaway.

50 knew there were cameras all over the store, so catching a body in a store was a death wish. The store owner was already down the street, running from the mayhem.

Once 50 got in the car, he pulled off without getting his snacks, seeing Racks come out the store in his rearview mirror.

Now 50 had another nigga to add to his shit list.

***

Bad News, Virginia

The chief of police, who was Captain Cole's boss, was cold because he had a stack of reports saying Cole was arrested in an assault on local drug dealers.

Cap. Cole even made the newspaper. This was why the chief of police was on his ass all morning. Cap. Cole walked back to his office, shaking his head. He hated snitches, especially the drug-dealing type.

Chapter 29

Dale City, Virginia

Ja was sitting outside of the apartment building in a Cadillac, watching an apartment window on the second floor, which belonged to Tank Brim's girlfriend.

Racks and Ja came up with the idea to take out 50 and Tank Brim then focus on Capo, Pookie, and Lil' PJ, because Capo and them had so many ops, ain't no telling who was gonna kill them.

Tank Brim ain't stopped by all day. It was 10 p.m. and he was ready to leave. He had been parked there since 9 a.m.

Ja opened up his glove compartment and grabbed his pistol.

Star was putting on her left heel looking at herself in the mirror, admiring her perfectly shaped body in her dress.

Star was short, dark skin, and very attractive. She was considered a dime piece with class.

Her and Tank Brim had been fucking around for a few months now, and he was all she could think about.

Tonight they planned to go out to a new club in Richmond, and they were going to spend the night at a fancy hotel.

She heard a knock at the door and got excited, knowing it was her boo. Even though he was an hour early, he was still here.

Star turned off the Summer Walker album on her stereo and opened the door for her man.

"Daddy..." She stood there smiling, but when she saw a man with a gun pointed at her face, she thought she was dreaming.

Boom!!
Boom!!

Two bullets ripped through her forehead as her body hit the ground before Ja walked off.

***

Ten minutes later

Tank Brim wanted to surprise Star by showing up early and giving her a new diamond necklace he bought for her, to show her he was trying to get serious about her.

He saw her door was open, but when he got closer he saw Star lying dead in a pool of blood under her head.

Tank Brim shed a tear and turned to leave. It seemed like everyone he cared for was dying, and he knew it was his fault.

***

Sux 2 Prison, VA
Two Months Later

Months ago, Don beat his fighting ticket, so he was able to come back to his unit. Last week, the kid from New York he helped was now his celly after he got out the box, "Special Housing Unit," for another stabbing he did.

His celly and half the unit were outside at a basketball game hosted by his dad, Rich.

Don was planning a way to get his dad back for what he tried to do. The part that was killing him was how Rich was playing a game so smooth and covering his ass.

Every time they talked, Rich always talked about going home, and if they didn't already know what he knew, that he would have been told. Rich was trying to get home the right way.

Don had a couple of ounces of dog food, but he was giving that shit to niggas he be fucking with. Most everyone in the unit were dope fiends or K-2 junkies.

Nobody knew about Don's plan to handle his rat ass father, but Don learned to never wear his emotions on his sleeve.

***

Hampton, Virginia

50 and Tank Brim were driving the big body Lincoln Town Car with the large trunk space.

They were driving into the country. Everywhere, all they saw were cows and farms.

An hour ago, the men were coming out of the strip club with a stripper they had to kill, while kidnapping Racks after hitting him with the car.

"This is going to be fun," Tank Brim said, hearing Racks' moans in the trunk as they pulled onto a small, dirt country road on the side of a highway.

50 parked and got out with Tank Brim to pop the trunk.

"Take the tape off his mouth," 50 told Tank Brim.

"Nigga, he ain't fitting bite me. You put it on him," Tank Brim replied.

"Ahhh... Please, I didn't do shit to y'all niggas!" Racks shouted.

"You just tried to kill me." 50 laughed while Tank Brim dragged Racks out the trunk and tossed him on the floor, tied up. Tank Brim poured gas on his body, a whole gallon, as Racks cried and screamed. When Tank lit a lighter and napkin, Racks' body went up in flames as he screamed until he was burned to death. 50 and Tank stood there enjoying the show.

Romell Tukes

Chapter 30
Miami, Florida

50 just left the car dealership from renting a Wraith for the week. He needed a vacation from the mayhem going on in VA.

Plus, it was Jazzy's birthday, so he wanted to do something special for her and bring her down to the beautiful city of sunshine.

Jazzy had been wanting to get her body done forever, and today was her big day. 50 paid for her breasts to get enlarged and for her to get her ass done by one of the best doctors in Miami, Dr. Miami.

"Babe, thank you so much for bringing me out here. This is the best birthday ever, I love you," Jazzy said, holding his hand as he drove the Wraith through traffic.

"I love you too, but are you sure you want to get your body done, baby? Your ass is already perfect. You don't have to be like those Instagram models. You're fine just the way you are, baby," he said, pulling into the parking lot of a doctor's office.

"50, please, I want to do this for me, so stop asking me that. I'm not trying to be no Instagram model. I got 300,000 followers on IG. I'm just being me. I just want to feel comfortable in my own skin. You wouldn't understand unless you was in my shoes," she said, tearing up.

Jazzy always had low self-esteem about herself since she was a kid. She always wanted to feel secure about herself, but she was never able to, so she always broke down emotionally.

"Okay," 50 replied, kissing her lips before exiting the car, walking her inside the doctor's office so she could get her work done.

***

Across town

Melly was in Miami for the weekend because the All-Star basketball game was being held in Miami this year and he was planning to attend. Melly was on College Avenue in the Chanel clothing store, picking out an outfit for tonight to hit up a few clubs in the city.

With so much going on in VA, Melly hadn't had time to enjoy himself and go out to have fun.

CL provided him with the best dog food in the city, so he was focused on building his own empire at the same time.

Before Big Boi got killed, Melly was starting to build his own little empire for his boy, but his death put him at a minor setback.

Melly finished doing some shopping for another hour and went to grab a bite to eat before going back to his hotel to get ready for that night.

***

Later That Night

50 pulled the Wraith up to the club, which was one of the many in the area. He hopped out in a Dior outfit with a .22 handgun tucked under his balls. 50 handed the two big, muscle-head guards $400, and they removed the ropes for him while a crowd of people got upset at waiting in a long line.

Inside, the DJ blasted Gucci Mane's new song, and white chicks were on the dance floor and wall shaking their asses.

The club was so packed people were asked to stand shoulder to shoulder. 50 hated being in a closed area like this, so he turned to leave, but someone caught his attention.

Melly was entertaining a Spanish chick at the bar, trying to get her to come back to his hotel, but she was playing hard to get.

Melly wasn't really a clubber anymore, but Miami was different. It was like a free-for-all, everybody was on the same thing.

"Come on, sexy, what I got to do to spend a night with you?" Melly asked her.

"Money talks, papi, me sorry," she said in her Spanish accent.

Melly smiled because now she was talking his language. He thought she was a classy bitch, but the truth just came out.

"I got 5000 for you for the night," he told her, seeing her blush.

"What we waiting on, papi?" she said, ready to leave.

50 was across the street when he saw Melly and a Spanish woman walking out the club and up the block.

50 drove the Wraith with the top down toward them at a slow pace.

When he got close enough, he pulled out his gun.

Boc...

Boc...

Boc...

The bullet hit the woman in her head and Melly got hit in his back twice before the Wraith raced off.

Romell Tukes

Chapter 31

Stafford, Virginia
Two Weeks Later

Capo was in his projects having a big cookout in the back section where the big gazebo was behind the basketball courts.

Today, everybody was out enjoying the hot sunny day, loud music for the kids, free food, and free liquor.

This event was thrown every year to remember a couple of good men that were killed in the projects.

"What's up, Capo? I thought you was going to stop by my crib last night," a cute, dark-skin chick asked, approaching him wearing tight little booty shorts exposing her little black ass cheeks.

Since what happened to his wife, he had been fucked up in his head when it came to dealing with women and relationships.

"My bad, Lil' Pooh, I'ma hit you later," Capo told her.

"Okay, but you know my deepthroat game is crazy, and I'm trying to taste that thing again," she said, flickering her tongue ring.

Capo knew Lil' Pooh gave the best head he had ever had, but he wasn't focused on sex right now.

He walked off, leaving her standing there horny and upset. Then she saw one of her exes and told him the same thing she just told Capo, and they went to her crib.

It was starting to get dark out, so Capo walked across the street toward the store, and two of his young boys were on his heels.

Tat...
Tat...
Tat...

Tat...

Shooters rushed out the store, but luckily, Capo saw them right on time. One of Capo's goons got hit up in his chest.

Capo shot two of the gunmen hidden behind a mailbox with his little man, and saw Ja among the other gunmen. Capo saw 10 niggas coming to him from his projects.

Boc...

Boc...

Capo hit another one of Ja's hitters, killing him.

Ja saw all the niggas coming out of Capo's projects with Dracos and AKs and took off, leaving his shooters to fight a losing battle. His men were all killed within seconds.

***

Norfolk, Virginia

Tank Brim was posted up outside of Ja's grandma's crib in a middle-class area, checking out the front door to see if he could get in.

This was the address he got from his boy, Nook, who said he used to fuck Ja's grandma, and he told him how much of a freak she was.

A couple of hours ago, he saw a thick, nice looking woman leave and come back with a young nigga who looked younger than him.

He walked up and played with the knob, which was unlocked. Tank Brim went inside and heard moans and screams close by.

Tank Brim saw Ja's grandma's fat ass bouncing up and down on a young boy's rod. Her ass was wide, fat, and jiggly.

Fuck this pussy," she cried as her juices covered his dick, while grinding her hips in a circular motion. She continued going crazy on the dick, until she heard the gun cock back.

When she looked back, she screamed.

Bloc... Bloc...
Bloc... Bloc...
Bloc... Bloc...

Tank Brim shot both of them, killing them both. When he saw Ja's grandma on the floor, she had the prettiest pussy he'd ever seen.

***

Sux 2 Prison, VA

Don was called down for a visit today. He didn't have a clue who was coming to see him nor did he care, he just had to get off his unit.

Every day there was a drama on that unit, and Don hated that shit. He never saw niggas gossip or be messy about shit like jail niggas. The only solid nigga in his unit was him, Knight, his celly from New York, and two DC cats.

Once he made it to the visit room, he saw 50 sitting there alone with an angry face, as always.

"50, what's up, bro?" Don sat down, taking his brother's silence as a sign.

"You killed K?" 50 asked with a stern tone.

Don knew the question would come one day, but not this fast. He wondered how he found out so fast and who else knew.

"Yes, I did. He crossed me, 50. He went against the code and put our mom and sister's lives at risk," Don told him.

"So you killed him?"

"That's not all. Capo was a snitch, 50. That's not in our blood," Don stated.

"How do I know you ain't lying?" 50 replied.

"Look it up, you're smart, but if you come up here for that, bro, you got your answer, dog," Don said, leaving and not looking back.

50 was in deep thought, but he wasn't even mad at Don no more because he would do the same thing. And 50 found out K was a rat, but he knew Don had other reasons for killing K, and for why he was in jail.

Chapter 32

Bad News, Virginia

Cap. Cole was waiting on Twin so he could pay his monthly fees.

These past couple months have been a little rough at work for him because his boss was on his ass.

All the killing around the city was only making it worse, so he was making every dealer he dealt with calm down because his boss was cracking down on him.

Twin pulled up in a hooptie with sunglasses on his face.

"Cole," Twin said, popping up with a brown paper bag in his hand full of money.

"Thank you," Cole said, looking inside the bag. "I know you're not dumb enough to short me, but I need you to be a little low key. The feds are lurking around the city. I don't even know what the fuck is going on, but it's some big shit going on out here. I've been doing my job, but with the feds coming into the picture, I can't do anything that's outta my pay grade, Twin."

"I already know."

"Since Bree left, the city went down. Why'd she disappear? Because she wasn't under arrest, the feds just wanted to question her," Cap. Cole said.

"I have no clue, but whatever her reason was, it had to be big." Twin laughed.

"I can agree with that, but what's going on here, bodies dropping, getting worse by the week," Cap. Cole stated.

"You're a cop, ain't you?" Twin said, walking off, laughing at Cole for trying to get him to spill the tea as if he was a snitch.

***

Fairfax, VA

The Maybach drove through the mansion gates with Lil' PJ in the backseat on his way to meet a plug.

Lil' PJ's old head, who just came home from doing nearly twenty years in prison, told Lil' PJ he knew the right person he should link up with if he wanted to get some real money.

His old head set up the meeting, and now Lil' PJ was here. Lil' PJ had no clue who the man was. All he knew was the mansion was lit up like a Christmas tree.

A big football player type nigga with dreads led Lil' PJ into the mansion's movie theater area where the boss was waiting for the young man.

When Gotti saw the young man come inside, he told him to take a seat while the movie *Belly* played on the big screen.

"You know why I like this movie?" Gotti asked.

"Why?" Lil' PJ replied, watching his favorite movie on TV.

"Not only was DMX a good actor, but it shows how they came up from nothing and made a way," Gotti said, "just like you, Lil' PJ. I did my research on you, and your name is heavy in these streets. I don't care who you were dealing with before me, but I want you on my team."

"I'm down to get some money," Lil' PJ shot back.

"I'm Gotti, and I'mma tell you this once, you get in, you're in for life," Gotti said seriously, letting him know death was the only way out.

Lil' PJ heard the name Gotti from somewhere, but it wasn't clicking in his mind because all the weed he smoked made him forget a lot of shit.

"Aight, dog, let's do it," Lil' PJ shot back.

"Let's go drink to success," Gotti said, smiling, welcoming Lil' PJ to the family.

***

Bad News, Virginia

Pookie's mom just finished her Wednesday night service with the other elderly women who worked for the church.

Every Wednesday night, she held a class of Bible study to keep the women within the church started on the Lord's word.

Her husband, Pastor Ryan, was at home sick, under the weather with the flu.

"Thank you for coming out, ladies. Have a good night, and may the Lord bless all of you." The basement door opened, and a gunman stepped in.

"Oh my god!" one of the women yelled.

"Y'all bitches better start praying," Melly stated.

"We don't fear you or your gun," Pookie's mom stated.

"Shittttt... Speak for yourself!" one of the women shouted, scared, in the far corner with nowhere to run.

"You must be Pookie's mom. You a tough little pretty bitch, huh," Melly said, slapping her with the butt of the gun.

Melly killed Pookie's mom first, then he shot the other women, leaving nobody alive when he walked out.

Romell Tukes

Chapter 33

Sux 2 Prison, VA

Don was sitting at the day room table playing cards with his Richmond nigga, Big Meechy, who had been in the prison over 12 years on his 45-year bid.

Big Meechy was a nosy prisoner. He was always in somebody's business, and he knew all the tea going on all over the prison.

"I ain't see you in two days, shorty. You've been in that law library a lot lately," Big Meechy said. They were playing a game of Casino.

"Just checking up on some new cases. Damn, nigga, you nosy as hell," Don said, laughing.

"Shit, being nosy might save your life one day, kid," Big Meechy told him, throwing out a ten of diamonds.

"I hear you."

"They got that bad little sexy bitch working down there this quarter," Meechy said.

"Who is that?" Don already knew who he was talking about. He just liked hearing all the prisoners talk about his wifey.

"Mrs. Washington, I heard she from Bad News. She the baddest bitch I seen come through here, dog, hands down. I jerk off to the thought of her every night." Big Meechy was serious.

Don had promised Nicole he wouldn't tell anybody she was his wife because this was her workplace.

They had sex a couple of times in the law library where she worked at now. Don heard prisoners talk about her all the time and laughed. The only person who he told she was his wife was Knight, his celly. And at first he didn't believe him, until he saw their pictures from the streets.

"She aight."

"Aight, you don't know a queen when you see one, but I wish I was rich. Your pops that nigga. I guess money talks nowadays," Big Meechy stated, seeing Don's face look confused.

"What do you mean?"

"Your pops ain't tell you? Man, bruh, your pops run this shit. He's had this little CO chick on his team for a long time. He even recorded fucking her in her ass, and I asked and got the head. Her head game is crazy. Even I saw that shit," Meechy said.

Don couldn't believe what he just heard.

"That's crazy," he stated.

"She is bringing him drugs, phones, and anything you can think of." Meechy hadn't even finished before he saw Don get up and make his way to the law library in the educational building.

Nicole was in a law library watching all the rooms to make sure no inmates started no bullshit. She did a double today, so she was drained.

She saw Don coming through the doors and she smiled, but the look on his face told her he wasn't happy.

"You fucking Rich?" Don asked her, seeing a surprised look on her face.

"Who told you that, Don?" Nicole looked around, and the hallway was clear.

"You fucking him, bitch?"

"Yes, I'm sorry, Don, but I needed the money. Please, just hear me out," she begged.

"That's my fucking dad, you dummy bitch," he revealed, seeing the crazy look upon her face.

"What!!! Oh my god. I'm sorry." She started crying before Don spit in her face and walked off.

Nicole knew she shouldn't have gotten involved with Rich, but he was paying her $15,000 for sex and to bring shit in each time. She had no clue he was her lover's father. She felt nasty.

She didn't love Rich at all. It was only a money thing to her, but now she regretted it all because she just lost the love of her life.

***

Virginia Beach, VA

Homo just copped 80 keys of pure dope from his plug in B-More. He had a cousin in Virginia Beach that could move weight like a bodybuilder.

"Yo, LA, don't fuck this shit up, dawg, or I'ma cut your black ass off," Homo told his cousin inside his crib.

"Nigga, when have I ever fucked up a bag?" LA said, looking at the 80 bricks of tan on the floor, thinking how long it would take to cut the heroin up.

"I'm going to Aunty's crib real quick, don't touch anything until I get back, dawg," Homo said, leaving the house.

50 saw Homo's Ferrari race off down the block when he made his move. It was a dark out, so his all-black outfit blended in good with the nightfall.

Homo told 50 he was going to get 80 keys and 20 was for him earlier yesterday, so 50 put a GPS tracker onto his car when he was with him.

50 knocked on the door, acting like he was Homo. He saw Homo and LA carry three big duffle bags inside the house, so he knew the drugs were in there.

LA opened the door and 50 smashed the butt of his gun into his nose.

"Ahhhh, shit…" LA cried out in pain.

50 forced his way inside, pushing LA to the floor.

"Damn, bruh, chill out. Dat's all you, dawg, I don't want no problem!" LA yelled, holding his nose as blood leaked out everywhere.

"Bag all that shit up, and don't get no blood on my shit, fuck nigga," 50 said, kicking him in his ass.

LA started bagging up the 80 keys into the three bags while using his T-shirt to stop his running bloody nose.

When he was done, 50 thanked him.

Bloc…

Bloc…

Bloc…

Bloc…

He shot LA four times in his face, then he hit the exit on his way to meet Tank Brim, who was waiting on him.

Chapter 34

Bad News, Virginia

Ja was at his trucking company waiting on Twin's arrival. Roc was in DC getting money, so he didn't bother trying to reach out to him.

Ja knew of Twin and Roc since they used to fuck with Bri until she ran off. The brothers' names were heavy, and he needed new allies, especially with Racks gone now. He felt like he was alone.

There was a little knock at his office door.

"Come in, bro," Ja said as Twin walked in with a red flag around his head, wearing a red Dickie suit with red Chucks.

Ja looked at him like he lost his mind, reconsidering what he called him.

"What's poppin', dawg, you been trying to reach me?" Twin said, sitting down.

"Yeah, it seems we both at war with the same niggas, and I thought it would be good to come together and clear the storm," Ja stated.

"I feel you, bro. I checked your resume out, but you could have been hollered at me and my bro. You wanted to get murked to reach out. I don't respect that, dog, because now you need aid," Twin said, getting Ja upset.

"Nigga, I don't fucking need you. I can hold this shit down myself. My resume is longer than you and your brother's!" Ja shouted, trying to control his temper.

"You might be right, but these little niggas up on you right now on that score board, and I know that, but I'mma holler at Roc when he get back from DC to see his outlook on this," Twin said, getting up leaving the office.

Ja was in flames. He hated when they just talked down on him. Now he was starting to run out of plans, but he knew he had to show his face to let niggas know he was here to stay.

Ja called three of his shooters on the phone, telling them to meet him in Stafford.

***

Stafford, Virginia

Lil' PJ and Capo had every hood in Stafford sewed up with the strongest dope in the city.

Five of Lil' PJ and Capo's workers were on the overnight shift on the block servicing fiends. They had a daytime operation and a nighttime operation so they wouldn't miss any money at all.

"This shit is dry tonight, cuz," Treat told his boy, Biscuit, who was sitting on the small staircase in front of the building.

"I heard Whitley and them bitches having a party across town," Biscuit told everybody.

"Nigga, they had high school bitches," Treat said.

"Bro, we all 19, what the fuck is the difference?" Biscuit shouted.

"Nah, I'm on some grown man shit, dawg. I'm trying to get to a bag. Y'all can go fuck with them little niggas if y'all want to, but I'm staying right here, folks," Treat said, seeing a Cutlass with tints pull up on the curb.

Biscuit knew there was something funny about the Cutlass because he'd never seen it before.

Four gunmen with AKs jumped out firing.

Tat...Tat...Tat...Tat...
Tat...Tat...Tat...Tat...
Tat...Tat...Tat...Tat...
Tat...Tat...Tat...Tat...

Everybody tried to get away from the .223 bullets, but they couldn't.

When all of Capo and Lil' PJ's workers were dead, Ja hopped back in the Cutlass, on his way to a couple more of Lil' PJ's spots.

***

Woodbridge, Virginia

Shay was on her way to meet up with her boyfriend, Melly, in some projects. She loved her relationship with Melly. It was different. She hardly got to see him, so when he told her to come out to Woodbridge, she was more than happy.

Life was ok. She was working and going to school, trying to succeed in life. Her brother, 50, reached out to her sometimes, but it was like the streets had a hold on her brothers.

She fought her way into the 4B building. She knocked on the door, and Melly let her inside, opening a bottle of liquor.

Walking inside, she heard loud music and saw six niggas smoking weed and playing cards, looking at her then back to the card game, laughing.

"Come to the back," Melly told her as she followed him to a room with a sheet as a door. There were three men, all naked, standing there. Before she could even ask what was going on, Melly put a gun to her head.

"Take off everything, and you going to fuck all these niggas, then I'll think about not killing you." Melly recently found out she was Don's little sister from a female he knew.

Shay was in tears, getting undressed and laying on the bed, as the men took turns on her. Then the niggas in front of the house also had their way with her. Six hours later, Shay was kicked out of the crib, sore, hurt, and bloody. She couldn't even drive home. She had to call a friend to come and get her.

Romell Tukes

Chapter 35

Bad News, Virginia

Today was Tank Brim's little brother's ninth birthday party at a big game. There were close to a hundred kids attending the party.

Tank Brim was drained from setting up the party, but luckily, it was almost over since it was close to 8 p.m.

He was there since 10:00 am, but it was well worth his brother's smiles. Since he was all his brother had close to a father figure, Tank raised his little brother as if he was his own child.

He and 50 had been so focused on moving weight in the city, he didn't have time for anything else. Ever since 50 robbed Homo, word was out that 50 and Tank Brim had them bricks in the hood for the low. Tank Brim told 50 he should have killed Homo, because a nigga like him always came back for blood.

"Tank, some kid stole my teddy bear," his little brother approached him in his kiddish voice, tapping his leg.

"So why are you still here? Go and get your shit back," he told him after seeing the sad look on his face.

Tank Brim knew his brother was soft. He wasn't a tough kid, but Tank Brim was trying to toughen him up.

"Ok," his little brother said, running off.

Thirty minutes later, Tank Brim and his brother walked out the game room.

"I left my phone on the table," his little brother said.

"Aight, stay right here." Tank Brim ran back inside, and it took him a couple of seconds to find the iPhone.

Tank Brim rushed back outside to see his little brother gone and nobody was around. Tank started yelling his brother's name, in tears, praying nothing bad happened, but he had a feeling it was karma.

Homo drove on the highway in a commercial van with two big men in the back holding Tank Brim's brother down.

Homo knew it was 50 that robbed him because he was the only person he told he was going to Baltimore to get some dope.

For the last week, he'd been hearing that 50 and Tank Brim had bricks in the hood for the low. Homo knew they were rookies because most niggas would have waited to sell the drugs they just stole.

He saw Tank Brim run inside the game room and made his move. He could have killed both of them, but Homo wanted Tank Brim to feel his loss.

Homo pulled over on a bridge and shot Tank Brim's little brother in the head before throwing him into the river.

***

Sux 2 Prison, VA

Don was out in the yard walking around with his celly, Knight.

"What's good, son? Lately you've been on some quiet shit, fam," Knight asked.

"Nah, I just have a lot of shit on my head," Don admitted.

"Shit, me too, my brothers up top in the Bronx wildin', bro," Knight said, shaking his head.

"I wanna ask you something, bro, and keep it a band, dawg," Don stated.

"What's up?"

"You got my back?"

"Facts, you my celly, bro, and you saved my life," Knight added.

"Aight, you the only person who knows this, but I'm telling you because I need your assistance," Don said, and Knight agreed.

Don gave Knight the whole rundown about Rich from beginning to end, and he couldn't believe it.

***

Norfolk, Virginia

The chief of police of Bad News was in the bar taking his last shot before he went home to his wife.

Outside, he made it to his pickup truck and saw Cole step out from behind it.

"Cole, is that you?"

Bloc, Bloc, Bloc, Bloc...

Captain Cole left the man dead on the floor with four shots to his face.

Romell Tukes

Chapter 36

North Bad News, Virginia

Roc just got back in town and he was back on a mission to finish his war. He met with Twin earlier, and he told him Ja wanted to link up.

Twin told him he was all for it if he was, but Roc wanted to make sure they were all on the same page if they were to team up.

Roc liked moving dolo or with his brother, because he knew if shit was to go to the left, he could trust Twin, but another nigga was a big risk.

He walked into the truck company to the back, looking for Ja. Roc was popping up. He didn't speak to Ja or nothing, he just wanted to see where his head was at.

Once at the office door, he saw it was cracked and Ja was yelling at one of his new employees.

When the worker came out with a mad face, he knocked on the door.

"Yeah!" Ja shouted.

Roc walked inside to see Ja smile, as he knew Roc would eventually come.

"Roc, what's good, player? Have a seat, I'm glad you got my message," Ja told him.

"I was out of town, but I'm glad I can be here. Your name is well respected out here, cuz," Roc said, making Ja feel special.

"Thanks, but I'm glad you're here. I tried to speak to Twin, but he's hard headed and not level headed," Ja said.

"I know, that's my brother. I know how stubborn Twin can be."

"I wanted us to team up since we're outnumbered."

"I agree, but what did you have in mind?" Roc asked, trying to feel his vibes to see if he was really on something or just fronting. Roc was ready to get rid of Lil' PJ, Capo, Pookie, and the 50 cat. They talked and came up with a couple of plans to see where shit goes.

***

Club Star, Virginia

Club Star was the newest club in Richmond and it was lit every weekend. The dance floor was huge with two bars, six VIP sections, two stages, and the baddest bottle girls.

Tonight, Roc was out with four of his soldiers enjoying the night. He couldn't even remember the last time he went out to a party.

Cardi B's new song blared in the club, making the wall shake as people enjoyed themselves.

"Yo, cuz, we got to start coming out here more," Roc's boys shouted over the loud music.

"Yeah, we going to come back next week, but right now I got this little bitch I'm about to slide in across town," Roc said, as he texted his female friend who was in town for the weekend from Miami.

"We going to head back to Hampton, but don't forget I'ma need 40 of them things tomorrow," Roc's boy told him, who he'd been cool with for years.

"Aight, just call me," Roc said, standing to leave.

Pookie just so happened to be in the area when he saw Roc's blue Lambo drive through the projects he was in with his cousin, Chain Gang.

Pookie was stalling him all night. He called Lil' PJ to let him know it was lite and on sight. The only thing Pookie was worried about was the police station down the block, but he knew he had to be quick.

Roc walked out the club, passing a crowd of people just chilling, smoking weed or cigarettes because the club was a no smoking zone.

Pookie grabbed his 100-shot Draco and climbed out the car.

Tat...

Tat...

Tat...

Tat...

Tat...

Tat...

Roc felt a sharp pain in his right shoulder, and he pulled out his Glock .45 and fired, letting off his Draco.

Civilians were trying to get out of the way while Roc and Pookie tried to kill each other.

"You bitch nigga, stop hiding!" Pookie shouted, firing rounds at Roc, ducking under a Yukon truck with rims.

Roc popped up and shot Pookie in his stomach twice, but Roc heard police sirens near them.

Pookie walked across the street holding his stomach. Pookie fired seven shots into one of the cop cars, killing one of the cops. Pookie dropped the assault rifle and fell out, trying to crawl, but the cops jumped on him, placing cuffs on him.

Pookie was taken to the hospital and charged with attempted murder and the murder of a police officer. He was all over the news.

Romell Tukes

Chapter 37

Sux 2 Prison, VA

Don and Knight were walking across the compound to Rich's unit, passing prisoners going to lunch.

The walk was a quiet one as Don and Knight entered Rich's unit. The metal detectors went off, but nobody paid it any mind because everybody was busy.

The two corrections guards were in the back office talking about sports and about what female CO had the best pussy.

"Yo, Ice, where my pops at?" Don asked an old head nigga from Richmond.

"He in da shower room youngin'. Where you been? I ain't seen you in a while over here, youngin'," Ice stated, sitting in front of the table.

"Yeah, I'm low," Don said before making his way to the shower room.

Knight leaned up on the wall watching Don's every move, trying not to draw any attention to himself.

Don walked through the double doors and heard someone singing. The steam in the bathroom made it very foggy, but Don was still able to see his father in the back.

Don pulled out a long, pointy blade with homemade grip in it and rushed Rich.

The blade sliced Rich in his side, making him step back ass naked and punch Don in his face twice, doing nothing.

When Rich saw who it was, he froze.

"Don," Rich stated.

"Rat ass nigga..." Don attacked him, swinging the blade at his face, cutting him twice, then he stabbed Rich in his chest and heart.

Don held Rich against the wall, stabbing him until Rich's body went limp.

Don had blood all over the shower room floor and himself. He left Rich's lifeless body in the corner and walked out soaked.

Knight quickly grabbed the blade from Don and rushed outside to get rid of it.

A couple of prisoners saw Don's bloody shirt but didn't say a word. Ice had a T-shirt on the chair next to him and tossed it to Don and nodded his head, getting up, making his way to his cell before the prison would be on lock down any minute.

Knight got rid of the blade, and Don went to take a shower and change his clothes.

As soon as he got out of the shower, the police were screaming for everybody to lock in and somebody just got murdered in another unit.

Don went to his cell and got dressed while the rest of the prisoners came inside from rec. Knight went in the cell with Don, telling him how over a hundred C.O.s and the medical team was in Rich's unit.

"Whatever happens, reach out to them numbers I give you when you get out," Don told Knight before he took a nap.

Three hours later, a gang of high-ranking police came and got Don out his bed and charged him with the murder of Rich. They placed him in the "Special Housing Unit" while under investigation. They told him he was the last person to come out of the bathroom before the CO. They found Rich's dead body. They also had him on video tape with a soaked T-shirt with red stain on it that looked like blood.

Don didn't say a word, he just wanted to go to sleep.

***

Arlington, Virginia

Pookie was locked in his cell reading a book from Lockdown Publications and Cash presents called *Gangland Cartel*, which was hands down the best hood novel he'd ever read.

He was trying his best to move around. After being shot up, he almost lost his life.

His charge was the biggest event of the year. Two dead police officers outside of the club. Pookie made world news, but the time he was facing wasn't worth the fame.

Three C.O.s came to the door telling Pookie he had a visit.

Ten minutes later, Pookie was behind the booth looking at his father.

"Son, how are you doing?" Pastor Ryan asked when Pookie sat down.

"I'm good, Pops, getting used to my new life where I belong," Pookie said.

"Son, nobody belongs in a cage. They made prison to break a strong man's mind," Pastor Ryan said strongly.

"Why are you here? I don't need the word of God right now. I need to get the fuck outta jail."

"Patience, son... I know everything you've been doing in the streets, and I will bring justice one way or another," Pastor Ryan stated before leaving.

Pookie went back to his cell thinking about what his father was saying.

Romell Tukes

Chapter 38

Bad News, Virginia

Pimpin' Zac was in his hotel with two white bitches who sold pussy for him. This was an everyday lifestyle for Pimpin' Zac, living hotel to hotel, selling white bitches to Johns who paid top dollar for the trailer park trash bitches.

Pimpin' Zac dealt with white and black women as long as they followed his command.

"Daddy, can we go get something to eat?" one of the women cried.

"Bitch, you better to chew on your nails or them thin ass lips," Pimpin' Zac said, counting money and mumbling shit under his breath as someone knocked at the door.

One of the girls went to answer the door. Before the door even opened up all the way, Cap. Cole busted in with his gun out, scaring everybody.

"Cap. Cole, chill the fuck out, bro. Put the gun up. I'ma have your money tonight," Pimpin' Zac said with a trembling voice.

"I've been calling you, but you got a new number, dick head!" Cap. Cole shouted.

"Yeah, but I was going to call you," he replied, lying.

"Oh yeah, what time you going to have my money?" Cap Cole asked.

"I got two whores coming back in the next hour. Don't worry about nothing," Pimpin' Zac said.

"Until then, one of you ladies come here and give me a blowjob." Cap. Cole looked at both women, who looked at each other.

"You heard him, one of y'all go ahead," Pimpin' Zac said, as the skinny, tall snow bunny got up and went to Cap. Cole.

She pulled out his dick and started sucking and deep throating him, banging his rod into her throat. She made Cap. bust a nut in less than 45 seconds.

Even Pimpin' Zac laughed as he turned, knowing she put him out of commission.

Cap. Cole was paid in an hour, but before he left, he had the skinny, tall bitch suck him off again. This time he only lasted 30 seconds, but she enjoyed it more than him.

***

Bad News, Virginia

Sunday service was just finished up, and Pastor Ryan was shaking hands and embracing his guests.

"Ms. Berry, how are you and your lovely sister doing?" Pastor Ryan asked both women, who were regulars at the church.

"Well, your speech was an eye-opener, as always, you never let me down," one of the women stated.

"Thanks, but if you two beautiful women will follow me, I want to show you something," Pastor Ryan told both women.

"Sure, why not," both of the women said, following him to the back of the church that was now empty.

"I'm sorry to hear about your wife, Pastor Ryan. She was a great woman," one of them stated as Pastor Ryan stayed quiet, entering a room full of swords.

"This is a little overboard to be in the house of the Lord," one of them said, getting chills seeing all the swords on the walls.

"When I was in the special forces, I killed a lot of people, but I eventually gave my life to the Lord. I always prayed I didn't have to go back to the old me, but once your nephew killed my wife, I had no choice but to crawl back into my old ways," Pastor Ryan said, looking at the older woman, who was Melly's mom's auntie.

Pastor Ryan quickly snatched the sword off the wall and swung it at one of their necks, cutting her throat wide open as blood sprayed everywhere.

The other woman took off running out the office down the hall in her heels, but Pastor Ryan caught her, slamming her to the floor.

"Nooooooo…" she screamed before he stabbed her in the heart. He dragged her body to the office and made plans to bury both women in the back of the church when the sun went down.

Romell Tukes

Chapter 39

Bad News, Virginia

Tank Brim was riding around the city feeling like he was the king of the city.

He had his little man, Scrap, with him riding shotgun, looking for bitches, in the luxury car Tank Brim recently copped.

Everything was perfect, money was racking up, and he was starting to see a big profit. The lick from Homo was big, but Tank Brim was on his way to holler at 50 about a plug in Richmond he heard of that was in the same blood set as him.

Last week, Tank Brim's little brother was found dead in the river. It was a big thing in the media.

Tank Brim was sick. He felt like it was his fault, hands down. There were only a couple of people he had in mind that would do some crazy shit like that.

They drove down the busy street listening to an old Young Jeezy album. Homo was in the Wendy's drive-thru arguing with the lady at the window over $8 in change.

"Bitch, don't make me run up in there on your fat ass!" Homo yelled.

"Nigga, you ain't running up in shit, bitch ass nigga!" she shouted.

"You think you tough, bitch," Homo said, as she went to close the window and run off, calling the police.

Homo pulled out the lot to see Tank Brim in his car bobbing his head up and down, with another nigga with dreads riding shotgun.

Homo grabbed his pistol and rolled down his car windows, to see Tank Brim and pop him.

Bloc...

Bloc...
Bloc...
Bloc...
Homo shot Scrap in his head four times while Tank Brim pulled out firing shot after shot at Homo, who pulled off into traffic.

***

Arlington, Virginia

Pookie was in his cell reading a magazine, waiting for lunch to come through the slide.

Pookie's lawyer came to see him yesterday, telling him he had the death penalty on him and.

A CO came up and slid a letter under his door, then shook her head at him.

This was Pookie's third letter he got. When he got off his bunk, he went to pick up the letter, which had no address on it.

Pookie opened up the letter to see the name Ivy at the top. As he read it to himself, he smiled.

Dear Pookie,

I'm sorry about what has happened. I've been seeing you all over the news. I know it's the wrong time tell you this, but I have AIDS and you were fucking me, so nine times out of 10, you got HIV. I'm sorry, I really love you.

Pookie had tears in his eyes as he filled out a sick call to go get a checkup.

He couldn't believe what he'd just read. He felt like he had a death wish over his head.

Pookie lay down crying, thinking about what his life was coming to.

***

Richmond, VA

CL's baby mother, Joanna, was leaving her apartment with her daughter in her arms, taking her to school.

Joanna was a beautiful black and Puerto Rican woman. She was tall, thick, and the mother of two young children, one who belonged to CL.

She was running late today because she couldn't find her purse, which was under her bed the whole time. She opened the Honda van's door and placed her sleeping five-year-old daughter in her baby seat.

Pastor Ryan watched Joanna come out the crib with her daughter. He was watching the crib for hours. He knew Pookie had issues with CL's people, so he was going for the main targets.

He climbed out his pickup truck and made his way to her as she placed a sleeping baby in the seat.

Boc...

Boc...

Boc...

Boc...

Boc...

Pastor Ryan shot Joanna six times in her back before killing the baby and walking off.

Romell Tukes

Chapter 40

Bad News, Virginia

Jazzy was in the bed with her knees bent to her chest while 50 long stroked inside her wetness.

"Oh damn, Daddy..." she cried out while he kissed her soft lips, nibbling on her lips until she hit another epic orgasm.

50's thrusts forced her into him as she screamed his name.

Jazzy wasn't done. She climbed on her man's shaft and rode the hell out of him in the reverse cowgirl position.

"Fuck..." she moaned in ecstasy as he hit her G-spot.

She was going crazy on his dick, dancing while he sucked on her titties that were swinging back and forth.

"I'm about to come," 50 said. Jazzy jumped up, placing his cock in her mouth, and slowly sucked on the tip while he busted up a thick load.

Jazzy swallowed every drop like it was nothing, then slurped up the little left on her chin.

"Mmmmmmm, you taste good, daddy," she said, laughing.

"Girl, you nasty as hell," 50 said, laughing, climbing out the bed.

Spending time with Jazzy was everything to him, but lately he'd been so busy in the street he hadn't made time for her.

50 had been on the manhunt for Homo while still trying to get money in the streets with the help of Tank Brim, who was going crazy.

"You coming back home tonight, babe?" Jazzy asked as she scrolled on her Facebook page, reading new comments on her posts.

"I don't know, but don't wait up, okay. I love you," 50 told her before walking to the living room to get his gun out the closet.

50 was on his way to go meet one of his workers to drop off five keys to him, then he had to go see Tank Brim.

Tank Brim was telling him about a new connect he knew of, and 50 was down to try.

***

Bad News, VA

Shay just came from having dinner at her mom Ashley's crib. She hadn't spent time with her mom in so long. Her mom was telling her how she got a young nigga she met at her job.

Shay was shocked to hear her mom was fucking with a prisoner who just came home.

Ashley told her how people could change, but you Shay wasn't trying to hear that.

She didn't tell her mom or anybody else how she was raped, because she was too ashamed.

She had a bigger problem. She was now pregnant and didn't know what to do because she didn't believe in abortions.

It was late, so she walked to her car, crossing the street, and saw a van creeping behind her.

The van stopped and she saw two men hop out dressed in all black. Shay quickly pulled out her mace and sprayed both of the men.

Shay ran off while the attackers, Roc and one of his workers, cried in pain feeling the mace burn.

***

North Bad News, Virginia

Next Morning

Ja was at work at his truck company getting a couple of orders and picking them up to be ready for the drivers.

He came in early today to get some work done. He'd been so busy focusing on the streets that he was neglecting his truck company.

Trying to get Roc and Twin to follow his orders was like pulling teeth because they wouldn't listen.

Ja told Roc to kill 50's sister so they could send a message.

Roc told him he was going to kidnap her instead and torture her, but Ja said that would backfire, and it did.

A man knocked on his door, scaring him.

"Excuse me, sir, but I was told you are the owner of this truck company. Is that correct?" the man asked, taking off his sunglasses.

"Yeah, I'm the one. How can I help you?" Ja asked, hoping the man was talking money.

"I need a couple of trucks to deliver something for me," the man stated.

"What type of things?"

"Bodies," the man said with a smile.

"I'm not understanding." Ja saw there was something different about the man.

"Yes, you do…" the man said, pulling out a gun.

Bloc…

Bloc…

Bloc…

Bloc…

Pastor Ryan stood to leave once he saw Ja take his last breath after he filled his chest with bullets. Pastor Ryan already stabbed the two workers to death on the dock area.

Romell Tukes

Chapter 41

South Bad News, Virginia

Lil' PJ was leaning on his car smoking a blunt of kush, feeling the power of the weed hit his lungs. He was in a state park early this morning waiting for 50 to arrive.

When he saw 50 pull up behind his car, he put the blunt out on the floor, blowing weed smoke in the air.

"50, what's up, bro," Lil' PJ said, who always had a good bond with him since 50's brother, K, was alive.

"You tell me, I'm here" 50 said, looking at the big rims on Lil' PJ's car.

"Yeah, but we need to talk because we have the same people in common, I believe! I think we can come together and gain control of the city because I've been hearing you and your man out here grindin'," Lil' PJ stated.

"Yeah, I'm finna get to a bag, dog. I fucks with you, PJ, but you know how Tank and Capo feel about each other," 50 stated.

"They're grown men. They got over it, trust me," Lil' PJ stated.

"I agree, and I'm down," 50 said, shaking hands with Lil' PJ.

"Good, you ready to put in some work?" Lil' PJ asked.

"Right now?"

"Hell yeah, get in my car. I got a location on Roc, but we got to hurry up, dawg." Lil' PJ said what happened in his car.

50 got in the passenger seat and put the Audi seat back.

***

Woodbridge, Virginia

Roc was staying at one of his ex's cribs in the suburbs while she was at work.

Today, Roc planned to meet up with Twin and ride through Capo's hood on a manhunt for him.

Roc hated he ever made arrangements with Ja, because he was trying to tell Roc he was calling the shots before he was killed.

This wasn't the type of teamwork Roc thought Ja meant, so when he heard about Ja's death, he was happy because Twin made plans to kill him anyway.

Roc was getting dressed in a nice Louis Vuitton outfit with the shades to match.

He grabbed his gun off the living room table and made his way out the door.

When he stepped foot on the lawn, he heard footsteps.

Boc...

Boc...

Boc...

Roc hit the ground and his gun slipped out his backside.

Lil' PJ and 50 were now standing over him.

"Fuck y'all hoe ass niggas, y'all know what's up!" Roc shouted.

Boc...

Boc...

Boc...

Boc...

50 shot him in the head four times before walking off across the street in the middle-class neighborhood.

Lil' PJ heard Roc was fucking with one of his little homie's sisters. This little homie hated Roc so much he gave Lil' PJ his sister's address so he could kill him, if he promised to do it while his sister was at work.

"That was easy," 50 laughed.

"This is only the start, playboy. Brace yourself, because we are about to do it big," Lil' PJ stated.

"Fact's, let's get it," 50 said.

***

Sux 2 Prison, VA
Three Months Later

Don was in the "special housing unit," which was the box, counting how many roaches he saw in the last hour. He was on number 157 and counting.

This was Don's new home since he killed his father a couple of months ago.

The prison charged him with the murder of his pop because he was the last seen coming out the bathroom before the police found Rich's body.

Don was reading the incident report and he knew they had nothing serious on him. He prayed he could get out of there.

A Muslim dude who was next door to him for killing a CO last year by stabbing him 16 times in his neck slid Don a Noble Qur'an, so he'd been reading that since.

Don's court date was in 60 days. He prayed for a way out of this, because he wasn't trying to spend the rest of his life in prison.

Romell Tukes

Chapter 42

Richmond, Virginia

Melly had miraculously survived the shooting and had recovered fully. Today he was at the city of Richmond car show, which was inside a large parking lot.

Melly brought out his 1967 Impala sitting on 32-inch rims with white pearl paint, white gutter seats, and a new engine built from the ground up.

The show was almost over, and he was laughing because he'd been out here all day.

He ran into 20 buyers, but he wasn't selling his car, ever. He really loved old school cars, especially muscle cars, which were his favorite since he was a kid.

Melly was preparing to leave, but he saw a familiar face standing a few feet away, watching his every move.

Boc...
Boc...
Boc...
Boc...

Pastor Ryan let off shots through the crowd and hit two civilians trying to hit Melly, who was ducking, going for his gun under his car seat.

Once Melly got a hold of his gun, the pastor let off 10 rounds, getting Melly in his back.

The police rushed the crowd and Pastor Ryan, and Melly took off running, leaving four dead bodies at the scene.

***

Bad News, Virginia

Jazzy just left work early because she wasn't feeling good at all, but she thought it was the lunch she ate.

Jazzy didn't realize she missed her period. She was far from green, so she went to get a pregnancy test and it read she was pregnant.

She was happy at first, then she thought about the type of lifestyle 50 lived, and she knew it wouldn't be a smart idea to bring a child into this world unless he cleaned his act up.

She made her way home with so many thoughts on her mind.

**

Across Town
Meanwhile

Cap. Cole was on his way to a lunch date with his daughter, who rarely called him or even acknowledged him for the past fallout.

Cap. Cole loved his daughter, but she was too much like him, hard headed.

Since he killed the chief of police, his days were back to normal, and luckily, the chief of police was replaced by a dirty cop.

He was 30 minutes late for his lunch date, but he didn't care. At least he made it, was his excuse.

Walking into the small restaurant, he saw his daughter sitting in the back with that upset book all over her face.

"Sorry I'm late," Cap. Cole said, sitting down looking at his daughter, Ashley.

"When are you going to tell your grandchildren who you are?" Ashley asked, to the point of why she was here.

Years ago, when she got pregnant by a black man, he disowned her. When it happened again, he cut her off.

"Soon," he said.

"That's not good enough. Your grandson, Don, is in prison with a murder charge from the inside. 50 is in the street and K is dead, so you still think soon will be good, asshole?" Ashley got an attitude.

"Ashley, just give me some time. I have a lot going on," Cap. Cole admitted.

"Oh yeah, I figured you'd say that, so I took it upon myself."

50 walked in and saw one of the dirtiest cops in the city sitting next to his mom.

"Mom, what is he doing here?" 50 looked at his mom.

"This is your grandfather, the one who was never around for none of you, and he was a shitty ass dad to me and my siblings," she replied.

"Come on, Ashley, you don't have to do this," Cap. Cole told her, looking at 50, who thought this was a joke.

"I'm out. I don't got time for this bullshit." 50 left, wishing his mother was lying, but he knew it was real.

"You see how you always run your own blood away," she said, grabbing her purse.

"He wasn't supposed to do it like this, Ashley, it's not right," he stated seriously.

"Tell me about it. Take care, Captain Cole, I'll see you around," Ashley said, getting up to leave.

Romell Tukes

Chapter 43

Atlanta, Georgia
Two Months Later

CL was chilling in his big Buckhead mansion with seven rooms, five bathrooms, a four-car garage, and four acres of land.

This was his new home until shit died down in VA. The city had turned into a warzone. And he knew, sooner or later, the past would be in town again.

Last week he threw a big pool party at his crib, and he met a lot of made niggas from all over the city of Atlanta.

He was supposed to meet two new clients from zone 6 tonight at the famous Magic City strip club.

CL loved Atlanta clubs. They were super lit and the dancers got naked, which was beautiful to the customer.

CL was laying in his California king-size bed with two strippers he met at Pool Palace. It was time for the dancers to leave, so CL woke them up and kicked them out the mansion.

***

Bad News, Virginia

Pastor Ryan was in the basement of his church cutting into new bodies he killed earlier today.

The two bodies were Twin's people. Pastor Ryan was on a mission. He planned to kill two or more people every day until he found Melly, Twin, and CL.

As he was cutting bodies up, he heard footsteps upstairs, which made him stop doing what he was doing.

Walking upstairs at church was dark and pitch black.

When he saw the red beans aiming through the hallway, he ducked out the way.

He knew there was nowhere to go except to his casket, but he knew the Lord had him covered.

Boc...

Boc...

Boc...

Boc...

Pastor Ryan saw two men drop to the floor before a drum roll of bullets came his way as he rolled across the floor, as if he was in training.

Pastor Ryan got flashbacks to when he was in the war.

Boc...

Boc...

Boc...

Boc...

Pastor Ryan fired three shots into one of the cop's neck, killing him.

Ten more shooters popped up behind him and shot him eight times in his back, dropping him, making him drop his gun.

Pastor Ryan was on his last breath while a gang of FBI agents surrounded him, watching him die.

The feds had a warrant for his arrest for killing civilians in Richmond at a car show when he was trying to kill Melly.

While searching the church, the police found six bodies in the basement of the church.

The media came through and put the scene on the world news.

***

Arlington, Virginia
Next Day

Pookie was in the day room by himself, watching the news with tears as he looked at his father's face across the screen.

Pookie was shocked to see his dad killed all them agents, and he was saddened about all the dead corpses found in the church.

Tears fell down his cheeks, because now he was alone in life with nobody by his side besides his homies.

Pookie was ready to go to his cell and sleep his tears and pain away.

***

Bad News, Virginia
Seven Months Later

50 was leaving his crib to go pick up some diapers and baby food. He and Jazzy had a beautiful baby girl, healthy and the cutest thing he ever saw.

It was close to midnight, but there was a 24-hour shopping center down the block.

50 and Tank Brim had a connect now, so they were moving weight all over VA.

When he grabbed his two and a half, a man popped up from the side block.

"Don't move, fuck nigga. I'll knock your head off your shoulders, hoe ass nigga. Turn your bitch ass around," the voice said.

50 turned around slowly, looking at Homo.

"Nigga, I'm supposed to be scared of you, you bitch ass nigga?" 50 stated.

"I've been waiting for this day for a long time." Homo pressed his Colt 45 at his head.

"Take your best shot."

"You real tough with a gun to your big-ass head," Homo whispered.

BOOM...

BOOM...

50's eyes widened when Homo's body collapsed on his.

"What the fuck?" 50 pushed Homo's body on the floor and saw Don approach out of the dark.

"Congrats on the baby, bro," Don said, embracing his brother.

"Damn, dog, I thought you were locked up." 50 looked at Homo's dead body, happy Don saved his ass.

"I was. I got out two weeks ago. Somebody took the body for me," Don stated.

While Don was in the box, someone admitted to killing Rich so that he could go home. Don wondered who would risk it all for him, and when he saw old head Ice, who was in the unit with Rich, he was shocked.

Minutes before then Don came into the unit to kill Rich, Ice went to take a piss in the bathroom.

When Ice told police he did it, they rewound the footage to see him going into the bathroom before Don. They knew there was a strong chance he could have done it. The courts didn't care who did it, they just wanted a conviction.

Ice was already doing a life sentence plus 325 years, so they weren't hurting him at all.

Don was released from prison two days after that, and he sent Ice a hundred thousand so Ice would be well taken care of.

Don and 50 headed across town, but when they got a call from their mother, the happy reunion was over.

***

Across Town

Meanwhile

Ashley was in her home on the floor, tied up with four men standing over her, all dressed in red with Timbs.

"Good job," Bloody said in his New York accent, taking the phone from Ashley, who was crying.

"Please, I don't even know what's going on."

"I know, but that's how it is sometimes, sexy." Bloody looked at his Rolex watch. They should be there any minute, so he ain't have much time.

Bloody was Rich's other son nobody knew about, because Rich got a woman pregnant before he moved to Virginia. Rich told the woman to get an abortion because they were only 15 years old. The girl's mom wouldn't allow that, so she had Bloody, whose real name was Brandon.

"You look like someone," Ashley told him.

"You think? How about my father, Rich." Ashley was unaware Rich had more kids. She thought that she was the only one.

"Got to go back to New York, take care." Bloody fired six shots into her frame, killing her.

To Be Continued…
A Dopeboy's Dream 3
Coming Soon

Submission Guideline

Submit the first three chapters of your completed manuscript to ldpsubmissions@gmail.com, subject line: Your book's title. The manuscript must be in a .doc file and sent as an attachment. Document should be in Times New Roman, double spaced and in size 12 font. Also, provide your synopsis and full contact information. If sending multiple submissions, they must each be in a separate email.

Have a story but no way to send it electronically? You can still submit to LDP/Ca$h Presents. Send in the first three chapters, written or typed, of your completed manuscript to:

LDP: Submissions Dept
Po Box 944
Stockbridge, Ga 30281

DO NOT send original manuscript. Must be a duplicate.

Provide your synopsis and a cover letter containing your full contact information.

Thanks for considering LDP and Ca$h Presents.

NEW RELEASES

MOB TIES 3 by SAYNOMORE
CONFESSIONS OF A GANGSTA by NICHOLAS LOCK
MURDA WAS THE CASE by ELIJAH R. FREEMAN
THE STREETS NEVER LET GO by ROBERT BAPTISTE
MOBBED UP 4 by KING RIO
AN UNFORESEEN LOVE 2 by MEESHA
KING OF THE TRENCHES by GHOST & TRANAY ADAMS
A DOPEBOY'S DREAM by ROMELL TUKES

3X KRAZY III

De'Kari

KINGPIN KILLAZ IV

STREET KINGS III

PAID IN BLOOD III

CARTEL KILLAZ IV

DOPE GODS III

Hood Rich

SINS OF A HUSTLA II

ASAD

RICH $AVAGE II

By Troublesome

YAYO V

Bred In The Game 2

S. Allen

CREAM III

By Yolanda Moore

SON OF A DOPE FIEND III

HEAVEN GOT A GHETTO II

By Renta

LOYALTY AIN'T PROMISED III

By Keith Williams

I'M NOTHING WITHOUT HIS LOVE II

SINS OF A THUG II

TO THE THUG I LOVED BEFORE II

By Monet Dragun

QUIET MONEY IV

EXTENDED CLIP III

THUG LIFE IV

By **Trai'Quan**

THE STREETS MADE ME IV

By **Larry D. Wright**

IF YOU CROSS ME ONCE II

By **Anthony Fields**

THE STREETS WILL NEVER CLOSE II

By **K'ajji**

HARD AND RUTHLESS III

THE BILLIONAIRE BENTLEYS II

Von Diesel

KILLA KOUNTY II

By **Khufu**

MONEY GAME II

By **Smoove Dolla**

A GANGSTA'S KARMA II

By **FLAME**

JACK BOYZ VERSUS DOPE BOYZ

A DOPEBOY'S DREAM III

By **Romell Tukes**

MOB TIES IV

By **SayNoMore**

MURDA WAS THE CASE II

Elijah R. Freeman

THE STREETS NEVER LET GO II

By **Robert Baptiste**

AN UNFORESEEN LOVE III
By **Meesha**
KING OF THE TRENCHES II
by **GHOST & TRANAY ADAMS**

Available Now

RESTRAINING ORDER **I & II**
By **CA$H & Coffee**
LOVE KNOWS NO BOUNDARIES **I II & III**
By **Coffee**
RAISED AS A GOON I, II, III & IV
BRED BY THE SLUMS I, II, III
BLAST FOR ME I & II
ROTTEN TO THE CORE I II III
A BRONX TALE I, II, III
DUFFLE BAG CARTEL I II III IV V VI
HEARTLESS GOON I II III IV V
A SAVAGE DOPEBOY I II
DRUG LORDS I II III
CUTTHROAT MAFIA I II
KING OF THE TRENCHES
By **Ghost**

LAY IT DOWN **I & II**

LAST OF A DYING BREED I II

BLOOD STAINS OF A SHOTTA I & II III

By **Jamaica**

LOYAL TO THE GAME I II III

LIFE OF SIN I, II III

By **TJ & Jelissa**

BLOODY COMMAS I & II

SKI MASK CARTEL I II & III

KING OF NEW YORK I II,III IV V

RISE TO POWER I II III

COKE KINGS I II III IV

BORN HEARTLESS I II III IV

KING OF THE TRAP I II

By **T.J. Edwards**

IF LOVING HIM IS WRONG…I & II

LOVE ME EVEN WHEN IT HURTS I II III

By **Jelissa**

WHEN THE STREETS CLAP BACK I & II III

THE HEART OF A SAVAGE I II III

By **Jibril Williams**

A DISTINGUISHED THUG STOLE MY HEART I II & III

LOVE SHOULDN'T HURT I II III IV

RENEGADE BOYS I II III IV

PAID IN KARMA I II III

SAVAGE STORMS I II

AN UNFORESEEN LOVE I II

By **Meesha**

A GANGSTER'S CODE I &, II III

A GANGSTER'S SYN I II III

THE SAVAGE LIFE I II III

CHAINED TO THE STREETS I II III

BLOOD ON THE MONEY I II III

By J-Blunt

PUSH IT TO THE LIMIT

By **Bre' Hayes**

BLOOD OF A BOSS **I, II, III, IV, V**

SHADOWS OF THE GAME

TRAP BASTARD

By **Askari**

THE STREETS BLEED MURDER **I, II & III**

THE HEART OF A GANGSTA I II& III

By **Jerry Jackson**

CUM FOR ME I II III IV V VI VII

An **LDP Erotica Collaboration**

BRIDE OF A HUSTLA **I II & II**

THE FETTI GIRLS **I, II& III**

CORRUPTED BY A GANGSTA I, II III, IV

BLINDED BY HIS LOVE

THE PRICE YOU PAY FOR LOVE I, II ,III

DOPE GIRL MAGIC I II III

By **Destiny Skai**

WHEN A GOOD GIRL GOES BAD

By **Adrienne**

THE COST OF LOYALTY I II III
By Kweli
A GANGSTER'S REVENGE **I II III & IV**
THE BOSS MAN'S DAUGHTERS I II III IV V
A SAVAGE LOVE **I & II**
BAE BELONGS TO ME I II
A HUSTLER'S DECEIT I, II, III
WHAT BAD BITCHES DO I, II, III
SOUL OF A MONSTER I II III
KILL ZONE
A DOPE BOY'S QUEEN I II III
By **Aryanna**
A KINGPIN'S AMBITON
A KINGPIN'S AMBITION **II**
I MURDER FOR THE DOUGH
By **Ambitious**
TRUE SAVAGE I II III IV V VI VII
DOPE BOY MAGIC I, II, III
MIDNIGHT CARTEL I II III
CITY OF KINGZ I II
NIGHTMARE ON SILENT AVE
By **Chris Green**
A DOPEBOY'S PRAYER
By **Eddie "Wolf" Lee**
THE KING CARTEL **I, II & III**
By **Frank Gresham**
THESE NIGGAS AIN'T LOYAL **I, II & III**

By **Nikki Tee**

GANGSTA SHYT **I II &III**

By **CATO**

THE ULTIMATE BETRAYAL

By **Phoenix**

BOSS'N UP **I , II & III**

By **Royal Nicole**

I LOVE YOU TO DEATH

By **Destiny J**

I RIDE FOR MY HITTA

I STILL RIDE FOR MY HITTA

By **Misty Holt**

LOVE & CHASIN' PAPER

By **Qay Crockett**

TO DIE IN VAIN

SINS OF A HUSTLA

By **ASAD**

BROOKLYN HUSTLAZ

By **Boogsy Morina**

BROOKLYN ON LOCK I & II

By **Sonovia**

GANGSTA CITY

By **Teddy Duke**

A DRUG KING AND HIS DIAMOND I & II III

A DOPEMAN'S RICHES

HER MAN, MINE'S TOO I, II

CASH MONEY HO'S

THE WIFEY I USED TO BE I II

By Nicole Goosby

TRAPHOUSE KING **I II & III**

KINGPIN KILLAZ I II III

STREET KINGS I II

PAID IN BLOOD **I II**

CARTEL KILLAZ I II III

DOPE GODS I II

By **Hood Rich**

LIPSTICK KILLAH **I, II, III**

CRIME OF PASSION I II & III

FRIEND OR FOE I II III

By **Mimi**

STEADY MOBBN' **I, II, III**

THE STREETS STAINED MY SOUL I II

By **Marcellus Allen**

WHO SHOT YA **I, II, III**

SON OF A DOPE FIEND I II

HEAVEN GOT A GHETTO

Renta

GORILLAZ IN THE BAY **I II III IV**

TEARS OF A GANGSTA I II

3X KRAZY I II

DE'KARI

TRIGGADALE I II III

MURDAROBER WAS THE CASE

Elijah R. Freeman

GOD BLESS THE TRAPPERS I, II, III

THESE SCANDALOUS STREETS I, II, III

FEAR MY GANGSTA I, II, III IV, V

THESE STREETS DON'T LOVE NOBODY I, II

BURY ME A G I, II, III, IV, V

A GANGSTA'S EMPIRE I, II, III, IV

THE DOPEMAN'S BODYGAURD I II

THE REALEST KILLAZ I II III

THE LAST OF THE OGS I II III

Tranay Adams

THE STREETS ARE CALLING

Duquie Wilson

MARRIED TO A BOSS I II III

By Destiny Skai & Chris Green

KINGZ OF THE GAME I II III IV V

Playa Ray

SLAUGHTER GANG I II III

RUTHLESS HEART I II III

By Willie Slaughter

FUK SHYT

By Blakk Diamond

DON'T F#CK WITH MY HEART I II

By Linnea

ADDICTED TO THE DRAMA I II III

IN THE ARM OF HIS BOSS II

By Jamila

YAYO I II III IV

A SHOOTER'S AMBITION I II

BRED IN THE GAME

By S. Allen

TRAP GOD I II III

RICH $AVAGE

By Troublesome

FOREVER GANGSTA

GLOCKS ON SATIN SHEETS I II

By Adrian Dulan

TOE TAGZ I II III

LEVELS TO THIS SHYT I II

By Ah'Million

KINGPIN DREAMS I II III

By Paper Boi Rari

CONFESSIONS OF A GANGSTA I II III IV

By Nicholas Lock

I'M NOTHING WITHOUT HIS LOVE

SINS OF A THUG

TO THE THUG I LOVED BEFORE

By Monet Dragun

CAUGHT UP IN THE LIFE I II III

THE STREETS NEVER LET GO

By Robert Baptiste

NEW TO THE GAME I II III

MONEY, MURDER & MEMORIES I II III

By **Malik D. Rice**

LIFE OF A SAVAGE I II III

A GANGSTA'S QUR'AN I II III

MURDA SEASON I II III

GANGLAND CARTEL I II III

CHI'RAQ GANGSTAS I II III

KILLERS ON ELM STREET I II III

JACK BOYZ N DA BRONX I II III

A DOPEBOY'S DREAM I II

By **Romell Tukes**

LOYALTY AIN'T PROMISED I II

By Keith Williams

QUIET MONEY I II III

THUG LIFE I II III

EXTENDED CLIP I II

By **Trai'Quan**

THE STREETS MADE ME I II III

By **Larry D. Wright**

THE ULTIMATE SACRIFICE I, II, III, IV, V, VI

KHADIFI

IF YOU CROSS ME ONCE

ANGEL I II

IN THE BLINK OF AN EYE

By **Anthony Fields**

THE LIFE OF A HOOD STAR

By Ca$h & Rashia Wilson

THE STREETS WILL NEVER CLOSE

By K'ajji

CREAM I II

Romell Tukes

By Yolanda Moore
NIGHTMARES OF A HUSTLA I II III
By King Dream
CONCRETE KILLA I II
By Kingpen
HARD AND RUTHLESS I II
MOB TOWN 251
THE BILLIONAIRE BENTLEYS
By Von Diesel
GHOST MOB
Stilloan Robinson
MOB TIES I II III
By SayNoMore
BODYMORE MURDERLAND I II III
By Delmont Player
FOR THE LOVE OF A BOSS
By C. D. Blue
MOBBED UP I II III IV
By King Rio
KILLA KOUNTY
By Khufu
MONEY GAME
By Smoove Dolla
A GANGSTA'S KARMA
By FLAME
KING OF THE TRENCHES II
by **GHOST & TRANAY ADAMS**

BOOKS BY LDP'S CEO, CA$H

TRUST IN NO MAN

TRUST IN NO MAN 2

TRUST IN NO MAN 3

BONDED BY BLOOD

SHORTY GOT A THUG

THUGS CRY

THUGS CRY 2

THUGS CRY 3

TRUST NO BITCH

TRUST NO BITCH 2

TRUST NO BITCH 3

TIL MY CASKET DROPS

RESTRAINING ORDER

RESTRAINING ORDER 2

IN LOVE WITH A CONVICT

LIFE OF A HOOD STAR

Romell Tukes